THE UNTIMELY CHAMPIONS

THE UNLIKELY DEFENDERS BOOK 5

LILY SKYY

First Edition: January 2024

ISBN 978-1-960207-54-8 (ebook)
ISBN 978-1-960207-55-5 (paperback)

Published by Books to Hook Publishing, LLC.
www.BooksToHook.com

CONTENTS

PROLOGUE

The White Forest was normally a majestic, beautiful, serene place located in the town of Montgomery. But today, the forest seemed to tell a darker tale, one of lost hope and impending doom. It was no longer beautiful and serene but eerie and burned. Unwelcoming. Foreboding.

Five figures emerged from the heart of The White Forest, each wearing expressions of exhaustion and dismay. Kaos, a manipulative and strong-headed teenager, led the group, his sharp eyes scanning the path ahead as he tried to hide the fear gnawing at him. Behind him walked Amberly, Rose, Trace, and Kire—the other members of the Unlikely Defenders. For these five teens, the fate of their realm rested upon their shoulders.

Their latest battle had been a bitter defeat. They had faced Rezin, a powerful alien-like creature, the last of Yash's Earth-linked minions, whom they were supposed to capture, not kill. They wanted to capture him and lock him away so that Yash could never reach them. But something had gone terribly wrong.

As they trudged forward, each member of the group bore minor injuries and carried the weight of their failure. The silence among them was heavy and suffocating, and no one dared to speak. Rose, the most familiar with The White Forest, walked ahead of the others until, eventually, she fell to her knees, too weak to continue, although it was she who was supposed to be their guide out of there.

As Kire and Trace raced to Rose's side, both of them placing one of her arms over their shoulder to act as her support while she walked on, Kaos's mind churned, thinking of the horrors that lay ahead now that everything had gone so wrong. He was not one to typically wallow in self-doubt, but this wasn't just a small mistake that could easily be undone. He couldn't shake the feeling that there was nothing anyone could do now; they were now allowing Yash to seize control of Earth. During the battle with Rezin, the minion had somehow become aware of their intentions. As soon as he seemed to realize he had to die for Yash to move forward, he chose the sinister path of self-sacrifice, ensuring Yash's malevolent wishes could finally become reality.

Despite his manipulative, cunning nature, Kaos couldn't help but feel responsible for the disastrous outcome of that battle's ending. Yes, it was Trace's sword that ultimately caused Rezin's defeat, and yes, Trace had been the one wielding it when it pierced Rezin's flesh. It didn't change Kaos's opinion—not that he was about to tell any of the others about it.

The horizon was dark as they walked slowly, weakly through the trees. Kaos wondered if they would ever see daylight again. Or if Yash would come and wreak his havoc long before then. He wondered if, any second now, Yash would appear, his ship, Chaos, taking over the sky in the form of a massive UFO.

As they all walked, Kaos noticed how slumped over and defeated they all seemed. He wondered if they all shared the same thoughts he did: they were doomed.

Kaos's thoughts continued to swirl. Someone out of the five of them had to think of a plan, even if it seemed hopeless. And he was the group leader, after all. So, as they walked on, he began silently plotting and planning their next move. But as he tried, he couldn't stop it as his thoughts wandered again to Rezin. To his final moments. To the glee in his eyes as he realized the consequences of his sacrifice. He was more than happy to do whatever he needed in order for his master to succeed. Yash, the dark force that had attempted to destroy their realm for centuries, now had the very real ability to plunge it into eternal darkness.

Behind Rose, still being carried by Trace and Kire, Amberly walked, her hands shaking slightly as she pulled off her magnificent shining gauntlet. There was something about her expression that the others weren't wearing. She almost seemed to be in a bit of a trance. As if she were still seeing things that were not there.

Through the canopy of trees, Kaos briefly looked up to see the moon's glow before he looked back at his teammates, their faces weary. Their realm needed them now more than ever, but they also seemed further apart from each other than ever. There couldn't be a more inconvenient time for that to be the case. Their world was seconds away from ending, and they needed their gifts to save everyone more than ever. Why did they have to be the ones who were accidentally chosen for this? Why did a group of kids, all so different, have to rely on finding common ground in order to be able to save everyone? As Kaos stared, first at Amberly and then at Trace, he feared the worst. And the worst was what was probably the closest to the truth.

They were never going to get along.

1

The moon hung low in the sky as the group of teenagers emerged from The White Forest, their breathing still uneasy from the intensity of the battle they had just fought. Shadows of trees and shrubbery moved around them, all of them too tired to be as fully aware of their surroundings as they needed to be.

Kaos, his tall, slender figure moving with an air of confidence despite how tired he was, now led the way since they were out of the forest. His slicked-back hair gleamed in the light of the moon, looking close to perfect even though he had just been in a battle. His menacing stare swept over the group, ensuring that they were all accounted for for the hundredth time since they left the cave. He wanted to be sure to play his part as the leader well. It didn't matter if he didn't get along with pretty much everyone on his team. He was in charge, and it was part of his responsibility to look out for everyone.

Amberly, a stunning girl with blonde hair cascading like a golden waterfall, walked beside Trace, a fact that Kaos noticed bitterly. Her blue eyes, usually filled with a fiery spark of life, were still haunted by the horrors she had witnessed during the battle.

Her usually graceful movements that emanated confidence and a hint of defiance, as if daring anyone to challenge her, made her now seem as if she'd do what anyone told her.

Kaos's heart clenched as he observed Amberly. Sure, he had only gotten to know her because she used to be his best friend's girlfriend, but he had grown close to her during that time. Now, the conflict between them had him pushing to maintain his cocky facade.

I don't have feelings for Amberly, he told himself. But it was pointless—he just couldn't bear to let his guard down and risk rejection, but in reality, he very much liked her.

Rose, the quiet and quirky girl of the group, held tightly onto Kire, her boyfriend, Trace having released her when she told him she didn't need *both* of their help to walk. Though not conventionally beautiful, Charlie Rose was gentle and compassionate, and even though she was kind of weird, it was also kind of impossible not to like her.

Kire, who walked with a slight limp even though he was helping his girlfriend stay upright as well, *could* be seen as the brain of the group if it wasn't for the fact that Kaos was equally as intelligent. Kire used to be a loser, but then he started playing soccer, and suddenly, girls loved him. And even though he could have probably had his pick of the litter, he chose Rose and wanted Rose only. His eyes rarely strayed from her, and he was always ready to support her, especially in times like now, when she was weakened from the battle. For whatever reason, it was always Rose who suffered the most when their gifts didn't work right together.

Trace, who was supposed to be Kaos's best friend, towered over the others, his muscular build casting a large shadow on the ground below them as they walked. He and Kaos used to be an unstoppable force at their high school, but that had since changed. Unlike Kaos, Trace no longer seemed interested in ruling the school. In putting other kids down. In fighting—fighting at St. Bernard High, anyway. When it came to defending the earth, Trace fought like no one else. He had once been Amberly's boyfriend, but his heart no longer belonged to her, whether he or Amberly wanted it to or not.

As they walked with no particular destination in mind, Kaos with no idea what time it was, the group fell into hushed conversation about their bewilderment over Rezin uncovering their secret plan. Everyone except for Kaos, who stayed silent.

He desperately wanted to talk to Amberly, to offer comfort and solace, but the revelation that he was responsible for her breakup with Trace had created a wall between them.

She can't stay mad at me forever, he thought to himself as they walked. *She has to get over it eventually and realize they would have broken up soon enough anyway.*

Kaos took a deep breath and mustered the courage to approach Amberly despite the tension between them. "Hey, are you okay?" he asked, his voice softer than usual. It was a tone only ever reserved for her.

Amberly's blue eyes stared at him, filled with anger and pain. "Why do you care, Kaos? You don't care when people are hurt. You don't care when you're the one who hurt them."

Kaos's defenses rose instantly, his cocky ways slipping back into place. "Oh, come on, Amber. Don't make *me* the villain here. We all made choices. I don't know what Trace has you thinking, but I never explicitly told either of you that you should break up. *You guys made that decision.*"

Still, in Kaos's head, he had other thoughts about it.

He had long suppressed his feelings for Amberly. She was his best friend's girlfriend, for one. Two, Kaos didn't get into relationships. Kaos wasn't mushy. He didn't fall in love. He didn't need anyone but himself. And yet, he *was* responsible for the breakup. Because he *did* drive both of them apart from each other. What Amberly needed was someone to be there for her when her mother died. What Kaos told Trace was that Amberly wanted space. What Trace wanted was to be there for Amberly. To be able to comfort her, talk to her, and care for her. What Kaos told Amberly was that Trace didn't like Amberly anymore because her mother's death had changed her.

Still, even to himself, he tried to deny any emotions, pretending that his heart was untouchable.

I'm Kaos, and I don't fall in love.

They entered a random neighborhood, Rose falling again as they turned a corner. Kaos, who was closer to her at this time than Trace was, had a quick reaction to catch her elbow and stop her from hitting the ground while Kire was brought down with her.

Despite her exhaustion, Rose still managed to give Kaos a small smile of gratitude. "Thanks," she said, turning to help Kire get back to his feet next. As the two checked on each other, Kaos couldn't help but watch the tenderness between them. He knew that Kire was fully invested in their relationship, and his feelings for Rose were genuine and deep.

I don't want that, he told himself. Their displays of affection are sickening.

"Do you guys maybe think somebody *told* Rezin? Somehow?" Trace asked. "I just... I don't get it. He knew what he was doing when he appeared in front of my sword like that."

"What if it was the new Albus?" Amberly asked. "He's not quite like *our* Albus, is he? I don't know. I sort of get a bad vibe about him."

"Guys, it doesn't matter *how* Rezin found out," Kaos said, regaining his composure. "What matters now is that Yash can get to Earth, and we need to be ready for whatever he throws our way."

It didn't matter that they all had their issues. It didn't matter that his two best friends were mad at him. He needed to be the group's leader. It was his job.

Still in front of the group, Kaos turned and started walking backward so he could face everyone as he addressed them. "I think we all should head back to my place for the night. We need to discuss the next course of action. Strategies. A plan. A timeline.

Something. It is important that we are together as much as possible from now on and that we always carry our gifts with us. We never know when things are going to get... bad."

"Isn't there somewhere else we can go?" Trace groaned like the last thing he wanted to do was step foot in the place where he caught Amberly and Kaos secretly hanging out together.

"I don't know. Can *you* think of a place?" Kaos deadpanned.

Rose's quiet voice spoke with determination. "We can't let our abilities fail us again. We need to be together to make our gifts work. Let's just go to Kaos's. I am sick of feeling like this every time we fight. And I don't think anyone else's house would make sense."

"She's right," Amberly agreed, not looking at anyone. "Trace's mom is sick. My aunt's house is too small, and we would wake Aunt Lydia instantly. Kire's dad is crazy, and Rose..."

Rose finished for her since it was clear Amberly didn't know Rose well enough to know the exact reason why her house wouldn't work. "And my parents would never allow me to have you guys over. So, to Kaos's, shall we?"

Kaos shot Rose a grateful look, thinking they were making quite the pair of unlikely allies at the present moment. Usually, Kaos couldn't care less about Rose, and he was pretty certain the feeling was mutual on her part.

Everyone changed directions sharply and began walking in the direction of Kaos's house.

"It would be really nice right about now if your car hadn't been turned into a large pile of scrap metal right about now," Kire said as he continued walking with Rose, straining his voice a bit. Rose pulled herself away from him.

"I'm fine," she told him. "I can walk on my own."

"You're just going to collapse again," Kaos said when he turned around and looked at her again. She was white as a ghost. He nodded his head at Trace. "At least keep an eye on her, will you?"

Trace nodded, but he looked livid to be doing anything Kaos wanted. Still, he stepped behind Rose, ready to be there in case she needed a hand again. And without needing to help her walk, Kire was free to limp on his own, squeezing his eyes shut in pain as he did so.

Kaos turned back around, still leading the group to his house. He hadn't even seen Kire get hurt during the battle. How had it happened when he had Halo as his shield? When had it happened? It had just been one—Rezin—against five—the Defenders. Had Rezin been somehow able to attack all of them at the same time, all in different ways?

Kaos didn't want to think about the battle and what had happened during it. But he had no choice. Especially when, behind him, the gang wouldn't stop wondering aloud how Rezin had figured out their plan. He went along with it and said the same thing as everyone else, of course—that he didn't know how Rezin figured it out either.

Yet, in the depths of his thoughts, he couldn't escape the truth. Back inside that cave, Kaos had used his crown to try to see the inside of Rezin's head. He had done it many times before, and he had even been successful a few of those times. He hadn't thought this time would be any different. It would either work or it wouldn't. Kaos hadn't even considered that there was the possibility of a third option happening when he tried to see inside Rezin's mind. And it was this very third scenario that had occurred this time.

Kaos's mind had been flooded with indescribable pain, as if every single one of his brain cells had been lit on fire. In that moment of agony, he had felt an inexplicable connection with Rezin. It was as if their minds had merged, somehow, someway. Like maybe they had gone for each other's thoughts at the same exact time, and the result of that was their two minds colliding in the most painful way possible. And as soon as it happened, when Kaos was on his knees, screaming at the top of his lungs because the pain was too much and he'd rather be dead than feel it, he knew. It didn't matter how he knew; all that mattered was that he knew. Because of Kaos.

Rezin had discovered their plan.

It was Kaos who had allowed Rezin to gain the upper hand, and now Rezin's sacrifice had given Yash the power to reach their realm. To destroy it. Kaos wanted to forget it happened. He didn't want to feel this way. It was a sensation he wasn't used to feeling.

Kaos was full of guilt. It was so heavy he thought he might get crushed under its weight.

For now, he could keep up the lie. He could pretend to be just as clueless as everyone else was. Eventually, however, they would figure it out. He knew that the truth of Rezin's discovery would come to light, and he dreaded the moment when his team would learn that it was his fault their secret had been exposed.

2

Approaching Kaos's obscenely large and ostentatious home, some of the teens paused at the bottom of the hill it sat on, awestruck. Its grandeur was like nothing most of them were used to. Kaos's parents were rich, and Kaos was a very spoiled only child.

"You like what you see?" Kaos called to Kire and Rose, who were still staring up at the place as he walked ahead. Then he motioned with his head for them to move along. "Hurry up; we need to take cover indoors."

Up the steeply inclined driveway and at the end of the path wrapping around the front porch, the grand entrance appeared before them, adorned with intricately carved stone pillars the height of multiple stories. The sheer size and opulence of the mansion made Kaos swell with pride. Sure, he hadn't done anything to get his parents a house like this, but it was his house, and he loved that others were jealous of it.

The front door, made of rich mahogany, swung open with a slight creak as Kaos proudly ushered them inside. The interior of the mansion was just as breathtaking as its exterior. The foyer was filled with elegant marble flooring, and a massive, shimmering, *expensive* chandelier hung from the ornately decorated ceiling, casting a soft, warm glow over their surroundings.

Rose's big eyes widened even more as she took in the glamorous interior. "I don't even know if I should be in here. I might break something, and chances are it will be something that costs more than my parents make in a year—*combined*. Your house is way too nice."

Kaos couldn't help but smirk, relishing the chance to show off his family's wealth and status. "Of course it is. Welcome to the Palace of Miles," he boasted, his voice dripping with pleasure.

As they made their way through the mansion, the luxurious decor continued to impress the others, even Trace and Amberly, who had already been inside the home several times before. The living room boasted plush velvet sofas with golden throw pillows and expensive artwork hung on the walls.

Following Kaos into the kitchen, Rose and Kire gawked at the state-of-the-art appliances and gleaming marble countertops. Kaos gestured to the fully stocked fridge, filled with a variety of snacks and drinks. "Help yourselves, my parents won't care. They're probably sound asleep in their massive bedroom on the other side of the house." He watched as Rose and Kire exchanged glances, looks of awe and slight discomfort on their faces, probably at the stark contrast between their own homes and Kaos's mansion. He doubted they had ever been anywhere this nice before, and they probably felt like complete losers, just as Amberly and Trace had the first few times they came over.

After everyone helped themselves to snacks and drinks that would refuel and replenish their tired bodies, the group moved toward the game room, where Kaos opened the door to reveal a teenage dream come true. The game room was a massive space filled with the latest gaming consoles, a huge flat-screen TV, and shelves upon shelves of video games. There were signed, framed posters on the wall, two rows of theater seating in front of the TV, a pool table, multiple old arcade games in excellent condition, and several tables and chairs as if there could be an entire classroom full of kids being entertained inside, and in the back of the room was another sitting area that looked just as large as the living room by the entrance had been.

Kire's eyes lit up at the sight of the gaming setup, and he excitedly grabbed a controller, his hurt knee suddenly forgotten. "This is insane! You've got every game imaginable!" he exclaimed.

Kaos simply shrugged, trying to appear nonchalant about his gaming haven so he didn't come off as nerdy as Kire was currently behaving. "Yeah, my parents just keep buying me them. Helps me relax after dealing with all the realm-saving stuff," he said, feigning modesty.

Kire dropped the controller when he saw Rose struggling, and he and Trace helped her down into a plush armchair. Rose's fingers traced the ornate carvings on the armrest, blinking slowly. "This is too pretty for me to be sitting in," she declared, eliciting a snort from Amberly, who collapsed into the one next to her.

Kaos smirked, basking in admiration. "Not to brag or anything, but does it make sense now why my house was the best option for us to come back to?"

"You're definitely bragging," Amberly called him out.

"Agreed," Trace said before turning to address Kire and Rose. "Don't act so impressed. Seriously. It will get to his head."

"And it's big enough as it is," Amberly added. Kaos rolled his eyes and ignored them, twisting open a hydration drink and gulping it down. Then he joined the others in taking a seat in an armchair around one of the game tables. He liked having all of them there, not that he would ever admit it. But being in the game room with everyone allowed Kaos to momentarily forget the looming threats and challenges they were about to be forced to face. In here, like this, Kaos could pretend for a moment that. They were all just normal teenagers enjoying a night of games and laughter.

Trace handed Rose a bottle of water and a plate of snacks off the table, where he had dumped everything he had taken out of the fridge. "Take it easy, Rose. Dig in. You'll need your strength."

Knelt down in front of her, Kire was now dabbing at Rose's nose, which was crusty with dried blood, using a wet cloth he had grabbed when they were down in the kitchen. But he pulled away so Rose could drink some water.

"I'm feeling better, I promise," Rose said when she had nearly drained half of the bottle. "We have to come up with a plan. We can't just wait for him to strike. We need to be proactive."

Kaos nodded in agreement, forcing himself to tear his eyes away from Amberly, who still wouldn't look at him, so that he could get back to focusing on the task at hand. "Right," he said. "I felt like we were doing an okay job inside the cave until Rezin.... sacrificed himself. But an okay job barely worked against him. When it comes to defeating Yash, there is no way an okay job is going to be good enough. So, let's think about our gifts. We need to use our gifts strategically. What are some other ways we can combine them?"

Trace gripped the hilt of his flaming sword in its scabbard, like touching it would make him better at thinking of ways to use it. There was a fiery glint in his eyes as he said, "We gotta figure out some way we can make more use out of the fireballs this puppy can throw."

Amberly cracked her knuckles, a similar expression to Trace's in her sapphire gaze. "I know we can't use our gifts on each other, but maybe I could use my gauntlet to direct your fireballs wherever I need to," she offered.

They were off to a good start. Despite their anger toward him, Trace and Amberly still seemed willing to work with him. Then again, what other choice did they have in the face of impending doom? Kaos's mind was already spinning with possibilities.

"Rose's pendant, she can use that to create distractions or barriers," he said, pointing to Rose. "Depending on where the next battle takes place."

"And Kire's book... it is supposed to write the future, right?" Trace jumped in.

Kire nodded.

"If we can get a glimpse of what Yash is planning, we'd have an advantage. Think Halo will be useful to us this time?"

"Hey, be nice to the book!" Kire cried in defense as if Halo were a real person. Maybe it was—Kaos and the others *had* been sucked inside of it once. Halo's conscience was a bunny. "Halo has saved your life too many times to count!"

Trace ignored him. "Maybe we should have Halo keeping a shield around us at all times now. Don't you guys think?"

"It would drain all of the energy Halo can carry," Kire explained, looking disappointed that it couldn't be so simple.

Amberly's voice grew sharp as she turned her gaze to Kaos. "Maybe you can manipulate him into thinking we don't want to defeat him since you're so good at doing that sort of thing. So good, in fact, that you might not even need to use your crown to be able to do it."

So much for us working well together, Kaos thought, his eyes flashing with frustration and his pride refusing to let him admit his wrongdoing. "That's not true. Your relationship failed on its own, as I said already. It had nothing to do with me."

Trace, apparently unable to hold back his anger any longer as well, stood from his chair, his voice raised. "You're lying, Kaos! You manipulated *us*. You enjoyed tearing us apart! It was what you wanted all along! And there we were, worried about being the reasons why our gifts weren't as powerful as they could be. But this whole time, it was you, our leader, who has been causing us to suck."

"It's just like the new Albus warned," Amberly jeered.

Kaos's jaw clenched, his temper flaring. "You need to get over it, both of you! We have bigger problems to deal with right now. Seriously, how can you even whine about your pathetic little human problems when our entire universe is about to be destroyed, and we are the only ones who know about it and who can stop it?!"

Neither Trace nor Amberly responded after that, but still, the tension in the room lingered, and the argument threatened to escalate. Rose and Kire exchanged worried glances. Kaos didn't need to use the magic of his crown on them to figure out what they were thinking—that the situation involving the Kaos-Amberly-Trace love triangle needed to be diffused immediately.

Rose stood up from her resting spot, and as Kaos looked at her, he realized she had been telling the truth when she said she was feeling better. She had more color in her face. She didn't look woozy or winded. She no longer had new or old blood stuck to her previously ghostly pale face.

Kaos's initial reaction was annoyance at her need to give her two cents about their situation. He didn't want the lecture. He didn't want it pointed out any longer that he was the center of a huge issue the group was facing. He had never been seen as one of the quintets causing the issues, but now, it seemed as if he was the only one who was. And even though he was supposed to be the one in charge, the leader, now Rose, was trying to take control of the situation. But as Rose began to address everyone, he quickly came to the realization that she was worth listening to.

"Guys, we need to talk," she began, looking so exhausted it seemed almost as if she was resigned over it all. "This can't go on like it has been. We were given these incredible gifts, and maybe we weren't chosen for them specifically, but still, we have come further with them than anyone else who tried did, and we're a bunch of *kids*. I don't know. I sorta like to think it is fate that we were all in that cave at the same time and stumbled upon them. But, whatever. That's not the point of what I am trying to say. What I *want* to say is that we can't let our personal issues get in the way of what we're meant to do now that these gifts are in our possession.

"Remember when we first discovered the gifts? Remember how scary, wonderful, and unbelievable it all was? Remember how we were completely divided from each other? Do you also remember how quickly we came together and united to be practically unbeatable in the Albus realm against *so* many of Yash's minions? That brief moment when we worked as a team, and our gifts flowed seamlessly together? We were unstoppable. But then we let petty conflicts and misunderstandings tear us apart. And I get it. We're all dealing with our own stuff. Trace, I know it hurts that Amberly and you broke up, but we can't let that ruin our focus. Amberly, I understand that you're angry at Kaos, and Kaos, I know you have your own... secrets and issues that you'll never open up to us about. But all of these problems between you guys, between *all* of us—we can't let those things define us as a unit.

"We need to stand together and be a *real* team. Our world is at stake, and we *have* to put our differences aside for the greater good. But we can't do that if we're at each other's throats all the time. We need to trust each other and have each other's backs, no matter what. And I know it's not going to be easy. We *all* have our flaws and our issues, but we have to overcome them. Because we have to become a family. Not just teammates, but a *family*. I've never had a good family, you know? My parents have always preferred my sister over me—they've *never* really cared about me. But you guys, you might be... like, the only family I've ever really had, despite how awful some of you have treated me in the past. And I want us to be there for each other, no matter what. We can't do this alone. None of us can.

"So, for the love of *God*, can we please just put our differences aside and work as a team again? Let's trust each other and believe that together, we can face anything Yash throws at us. We have to be willing to sacrifice for each other, to be there when someone is down and needs help getting back up. When Yash comes down and starts destroying everything, the world is probably going to be a bit discouraged when they discover we're the ones responsible for stopping him. So let's show everyone that we're not just a group of teenagers with powers we don't know how to handle. Let's show them that we're a force to be reckoned with, that we can protect our world and keep it safe from *any* threat, including Yash. And let's do it together, as a family."

After Rose was finished, there was momentarily only one thing Kaos could think: *Maybe she should be the leader of The Unlikely Defenders.* He couldn't believe he was even having the thought at all. His usual arrogance had given way to introspection. But then Kaos felt that he had always seen the bigger picture and been able to look beyond it. It was Trace and Amberly who really needed to hear Rose's speech. They were the ones who couldn't let things go.

Kaos thought about the word he heard Rose use. It was one he wasn't sure any of them had ever said to each other before.

Family.

Rose's vulnerability in her speech struck a chord inside Kaos, and it was all he could do to pretend that it hadn't. Seeing her open up about her longing for a family, he felt the pang of... what was that? *Empathy?*

Yes. He was feeling empathy. Because he understood all too well what it was like to crave a sense of belonging, to yearn for a family that truly cared.

"You're right," Trace croaked. Kaos snapped his head to him. Was he seriously tearing up right now? "You're completely right, Rose. I'm sorry."

"Same," Amberly said, holding her head high as she looked at Rose. Kaos was surprised to see it. Amberly hated apologizing, and when she did apologize, she was usually much more dismissive about it. And to surprise him further, she even turned her head and looked at him again, this time with much less hate in her eyes. "Let's just move on from it, all right?"

Kaos cleared his throat. "That's what I have been trying to do this whole time."

"Right," she said and then looked at Trace. "All right?" she repeated.

"Yeah," Trace muttered.

Sitting back down, Rose looked at all of them with nothing but complete adoration in her eyes. Kire stared back at her with his mouth hanging open, seemingly blown away by her ability to give such an inspiring, motivational speech. And then, in that moment, Kaos realized something else—Rose was right about him too. He had to let go of his pride and face the truth. He had feelings for Amberly, deeper than he would admit even to himself. But the fear of vulnerability and the need to maintain his image had pushed him to keep his emotions buried beneath a facade of cockiness.

Kaos's throat felt tight as he swallowed back the surge of emotions. He wasn't one to be emotional. To feel empathy. Rose had a way with words to cause him to feel the way he did now. He looked at Rose, her eyes shining with hope, and as crazy as it felt, he saw her more than a teammate he was forced to get along with. He saw her as a real friend. Maybe even as family.

Because of Rose's words, Kaos made a split decision. He needed to let go of his manipulative ways. But being manipulative was part of Kaos's identity—he couldn't part with it entirely. For the time being, at least, learning not to manipulate the other Unlikely Defenders was a decent enough place to start. Only to the people in that room would he try to be honest and open, to be a part of the family they were trying to build together.

Kaos could tell the air in the room had changed and that he was not the only one deeply affected by what Rose had said. Others agreed with her. For the first time in a long, long while, Kaos felt as if they all were united, sharing one purpose as a group.

Sure, they were teenagers. And yeah, they were the only ones who knew of their realm's impending doom, and we're the only ones who had the power to even attempt to save everyone. Fine, they weren't as experienced as other adults, and they were filled with uncertainty about what lay ahead. But if they could keep up this unity, they would be stronger than anything that threatened them and their livelihood.

As much as Kaos thought it should have been he who made

such a powerful and inspiring speech, seeing as he was the leader of The Unlikely Defenders, he knew it wasn't the time to be petty. Besides, his pride had taken a backseat to the more pressing matter at hand—stopping Yash and saving their real—at least, for now.

"We need to work together," Kaos agreed with Rose, his voice deep and strong, "Just like Rose said. Our gifts are powerful, but they'll be even stronger if we use them as a team. So whatever problems we may or may not have with one another, we must let it go."

Amberly nodded in agreement, determination in her eyes that didn't used to be there. "You're right, Kaos." Kaos was surprised to hear it but tried not to show it. "We can't let our personal issues get in the way. We have to focus on being the Defenders. We're the only ones who have any chance of saving everyone. No one else even knows about the troubles coming."

Kaos had expected a bit more attitude from Amberly. He expected her to say something about how she was unwilling to put her anger aside. He expected her to demand apologies and explanations, both from him and Trace. He was relieved to hear her be so willing to listen to him and Rose.

Kaos nodded, trying and failing to meet her gaze once again. So, he turned to the others. "All right, then," he said, looking at Kire specifically. "Get out Halo."

Kire reached into his bag and pulled out an ancient-looking book bound in brown leather. The book had an aura of mystery and magic about it, and Kaos knew it held powerful secrets. Kire was the only one who could read or see the language it was written in since he was the one who selected the book back in the cave all those weeks ago.

"What do you want me to do?" Kire asked.

"Ask Halo for advice," Kaos said, his curiosity rising. "We need to know what to do next, how to stop Yash from destroying our realm."

Kire flipped open the book, his pen writing unfamiliar characters as he messaged Halo. The book responded, the letters forming unrecognizable words in a mesmerizing magical scroll across the page.

After Kire translated the words, he looked up at Kaos. "Halo says she can keep tabs on Yash," he relayed, his bushy brows furrowing in concentration. "We might be able to know when Yash is going to make his move."

Kaos felt a surge of hope at the revelation. Was it too good to be true? Things were never that simple. He had learned that recently. Still, having insight into Yash's plans would be a *crucial* advantage.

Then, just as Kaos almost expected it would, Kire's voice turned somber as he continued. "But... it's going to take all of Halo's energy. She won't be able to help us with anything else. Not until then, and probably not for a while afterward either."

Everyone was silent a bit. The potential sacrifice was something that needed to be deeply considered before they agreed on the best decision. They had come to rely on Halo's magical shield, which had protected them *countless* times. But now, they had to choose between having that protection and gaining the knowledge they needed to help them stop Yash.

Rose spoke up first, her voice oddly confident. "We'll find another way to protect ourselves. We have four other abilities between the five of us. I think we can let Halo preserve the energy until we get the answer about Yash."

Trace was the first one who nodded in agreement, and then Amberly reached out to squeeze Rose's hand in support as well—a rare sight to see. Amberly usually liked to keep her distance from Rose as much as possible.

Kaos took a deep breath. "Well, if this is what we need to help with the preparations of stopping Yash, then let's do it. She won't let us down, right, Kire?"

Kire and the rest of the group exchanged glances, understanding the gravity of their decision.

"Right," Kire finally said. It was official then. Halo was going to use any ounce of energy possible to keep tabs on Yash's arrival.

They no longer had the shield of protection, and they could no longer receive wise advice and future predictions from the book as well. It was a sacrifice they were willing to make for the greater good.

As the night wore on, the group's worries about Yash still lingered, but now they had the start of a plan.

Kaos, though still scared of what was coming, felt a small, feeble sense of hope. He felt as though he had just aged five years. He and they were no longer just teenagers; they were heroes ready to protect their realm with every fiber of their being.

Everything else—like the unresolved issues between him, Trace, and Amberly—could be figured out later.

3

As the first rays of sunlight began to peek over the horizon, the group bid their farewells to Kaos and left his lavish mansion. They had hardly slept and were going to attempt to get some rest before they went to school later and tried to pretend like the realm wasn't about to be attacked.

Kaos's mind was a whirlwind of thoughts after the others left before his parents even woke. He felt relief that they had gotten *something* done last night, but he was anxious about how it was all going to go down. Last night, the group agreed they were ready to unite and be one complete team, but was that really going to happen? What if Yash appeared, and their gifts were still weak because of the harboring resentment Amberly and Trace were keeping hidden inside themselves?

I wish I could just use my ability to read minds one time on them so that I could know, he thought to himself as he yawned greatly and tried to relax his tight, tense shoulders.

Somewhere in the echoing mansion, he could already hear the familiar sounds of the household staff starting their day, preparing breakfast, and tending to the needs of the house.

Knowing his parents wouldn't be awake for a while, Kaos took the opportunity to doze off for a couple of hours. In the quiet of his bedroom, he tried to clear his mind and free himself from the stress and worry. Eventually, he managed to get some shut-eye.

When he woke up, he found himself wrapped in a cocoon of blankets, the sunlight now streaming through the curtains. Sweating, his heart pounding from intense dreams, he threw the covers off and got out of bed. He couldn't linger on nightmares. Not when he currently lived inside of a *real* one.

Making his way downstairs, Kaos was greeted by the bright smiles of his parents, Alexander and Celeste. They were a fancy, well-groomed couple with striking features and cold, piercing eyes that mirrored Kaos's.

"Good morning, Kaos," his mother greeted him, giving him a brief hug. "How did you sleep?"

Kaos grumbled in response, not in the mood for pleasantries. He figured his parents were used to his moods by now, though. They probably thought it was just a phase of adolescence. They did not have a single clue about what he was really dealing with. About the weight he carried.

"Breakfast is ready," his father, Alexander, chimed in, motioning toward the dining room.

Kaos followed them to the dining room, wearing his crown as usual, which they had grown used to. His mom asked him about it not too long ago, and Kaos lied and said it was the "cool" thing to wear now. Crowns were the latest fashion trend at St. Bernard High.

Kaos's parents continued to shower him with questions as they sat down to eat, asking about his night and how he was feeling. Kaos responded with short and dismissive answers, his mind still preoccupied with the upcoming battles. There was still so much that needed to be figured out. So much they still needed to plan.

Noticing the short answers and that Kaos was even *more* moody and distracted than usual, his parents exchanged concerned glances, but they didn't push further. They had always encouraged open communication with their son, but lately, he seemed more closed off than ever. They expressed that to him not long ago. Kaos didn't care about making them feel better. To reassure them that everything was fine. It wasn't fine. Not only was their world on the brink of complete annihilation, not only had Kaos been the reason The Unlikely Defenders failed their last battle, but Kaos's attempt to win over the girl he was crazy about had completely failed, and he might have lost his best friend over it. Yes, they agreed to be a united team, but that was only when it came to being The Unlikely Defenders. Outside of that, Kaos wasn't so sure.

He couldn't shake the feeling of frustration and loneliness that gnawed at him. Anyone on the outside would think he was a spoiled, out-of-touch brat; despite having everything he could ever want, a great house, and a loving, hard-working family, Kaos was internally miserable. And if he was miserable, he thought others should be, too.

As breakfast continued, Kaos's parents continued to make every effort to engage him in conversation, trying to break through the walls he had built around himself. It made Kaos consider using his powers on them. Just to get them to leave him alone. He knew his time left with them might be limited, but he struggled at that current moment to feel anything other than apathy about it.

When it was finally time to leave for school, Kaos's mood had worsened. He felt a little ridiculous about it, as well as a bit confused. What had him so worked up? Things had gone well last night when the gang had been over at his house. They were taking steps in the right direction.

Kaos felt that this darkness inside of him was maybe something he could not control.

Kaos slammed the front door behind him, his mood matching the overcast sky above. He strode down the stone path, his black boots clicking on the cobblestones. The golden crown on his head gleamed, its intricate patterns shimmering with an otherworldly light. The crown granted him power beyond anyone's comprehension, but today, that power felt more like a curse.

As he approached his father's sleek, charcoal-colored car, he ran his fingers along its polished surface, suppressing a sigh. His own car had been a victim of an unfortunate accident, something of Rezin's doing. His dad's second car was a nice temporary fix, however. Once inside, the sunroof slid open smoothly at his touch, and Kaos settled into the leather seat, the luxurious material conforming to his body. He didn't care if it rained in there with the sunroof opened. He didn't care if he got in trouble for it.

The engine roared to life, and he accelerated down the long driveway, the gravel crunching under the tires. He turned up the radio, trying to force the music to drown out his turbulent thoughts.

It didn't work all that great; he still felt broken and guilty.

Arriving at school, he parked the luxurious car in a prime spot. Dressed in his usual all-black attire, he stepped out, his crown glinting, sunglasses on, even though it was still cloudy. Many of his peers gave him and the car admiring glances and whistles. Nobody questioned the odd accessory that was Kaos's crown; they saw it as a mere suitable addition to showcase his status quo. Only the rest of The Unlikely Defenders knew its true purpose.

Kaos's eyes flicked to the group of teens huddled near the entrance. Trace, Amberly, Kire, and Rose were chatting animatedly, their unique abilities hidden from the oblivious crowd. Kaos felt a pang of longing. But today, he wanted to keep a bit of distance between them. Today, he desired solitude. He wanted to be alone with his thoughts, to navigate the chaos pounding at his temples from inside his head.

He ducked into the shadows before anyone from the group saw him, wondering how he would keep avoiding them successfully all day.

As the morning bell rang, Kaos strode through the corridors by himself, feeling the energy of the students' minds ready to be read. To be controlled. Sure, they didn't know they had thoughts so easily accessible to him, but Kaos didn't care if they wanted privacy or not.

Reading others' thoughts would keep him from having to listen to his own. He spent the walk to his first class amusing himself by altering their perceptions. He made one kid trip and fall. He made another drop all their books and folders on the ground, causing papers to scatter across the tiled floor. He caused a couple to get into an argument. He made two senior guys start a physical fight. Everyone quickly gathered around and watched that one, but Kaos merely strolled on past, a grin on his face.

In the crowded hallway, he encountered Amberly. Their eyes met, a flicker of sadness passing between them. Amberly knew why he was avoiding them. Avoiding her. She looked as if maybe she wanted to say something to him.

He turned away, his jaw clenched, and continued down the hallway. He spotted Trace and Kire sharing a laugh, their camaraderie growing stronger, like Kire was becoming Kaos's replacement as Trace's best friend.

Then Rose caught his eye, her gaze understanding. She had always seen right through him, even before they had discovered each other's magical gifts. Rose was good at reading people. He wondered if she could tell how Kaos was feeling now. If she could understand why Kaos had wanted Trace and Amberly to break up. If she, too, could see that Amberly made more sense with him, not Trace.

In class, Kaos wasn't feeling any better. Impulsively, he manipulated them. To get their attention. To laugh a little louder at the things he said and did. To keep their focus on the coolest guy in school. But the more he controlled others with his special ability, the less he felt in control of his own emotions and the angrier he became. Why did he feel this way? Why did all this his words keep replaying in his mind? Was it possible that darkness really was consuming him?

Kaos leaned back in his desk, his eyes glazed over as their teacher's voice droned on despite his efforts to cause disruptions. The mundane lesson bored him to no end until, at one point, he decided it was time to switch from manipulating his classmates to manipulating the teacher.

With a sly smile, he adjusted his crown, its delicate patterns catching the light of the fluorescents above.

Before their teacher turned to write something meaningless and unimportant on the whiteboard, Kaos's gaze locked onto them. His mind reached out, sliding easily inside their consciousness and spreading like a spider's web creeping into every corner. With a push, he planted the idea he wanted them to follow.

Their teacher paused, the dry-erase marker hanging mid-air, as a strange expression crossed their face. Their thin lips curved into a small smile, and they turned to the class.

"You know what, forget about the rest of the lesson. Let's discuss something more exciting. Like... I don't know... How about we talk about everyone's favorite movies instead?"

Confused murmurs rippled through the room, but no one protested. Kaos's manipulation had been successful. He changed it up without drawing too much suspicion. The teacher wanting to switch topics was apparently perfectly reasonable to them. He leaned back in his seat, satisfied with his puppeteering, as the class launched into an eager discussion about movies.

Across the room, The Unlikely Defenders sat together, their keen senses registering the abnormality in the air. Kire's brow furrowed as he exchanged a concerned glance with Rose. Amberly's eyes narrowed, suspicion in them. Trace's jaw tightened, and his gaze was fixed on Kaos.

Maybe none of the other students noticed it, but to the group, the disturbance Kaos created was impossible to ignore. None of them participated in the movie discussion. Instead, their attention remained trained on Kaos and his glinting crown. The Unlikely Defenders knew exactly what he was doing, and it was very clear that they did not approve.

Kaos's control over the class was a display of his power, one that he honestly knew would strike a chord with the quintets. Still, it didn't stop him. They weren't his boss. It wasn't as if he was causing any real harm with his ability. In his opinion, he figured they should be thanking him. Instead, Amberly's lips thinned as she glared at Kaos. Trace's fingers tightened around his pencil, tension in his posture. Rose's expression kept changing between frustration and concern. She kept looking between Kaos and Kire as if Kire was supposed to do something about this.

Kaos didn't care. He was satisfied. And it radiated across the rest of the classroom, where his other peers were satisfied, too. In instances like this, the power was intoxicating to him, and he reveled in his control. Let The Unlikely Defenders silently condemn him. He would pay them no mind.

WHEN LUNCHTIME CAME, Kaos found an empty bench in a secluded corner of the cafeteria. He looked around, the chatter and laughter of his peers thudding loudly in his ears. Sometimes, he wondered if the crown controlled him. If wearing it caused him to want to be manipulative. He almost wished he could just release it and be free from its grip. Maybe then, there wouldn't be this dark feeling inside of him. One that felt as if it was growing.

He growled under his breath and shot up to his feet. *I am so sick of overthinking*, he thought to himself as he started walking. He spotted a group of students huddled together, laughing and chatting away. His eyes locked onto Jeremy, a timid guy who had often been the butt of his jokes in the past. Today, Kaos quickly decided he had something special in mind for him.

He approached the group, the crown's magic humming with what was probably a dark energy. Letting the feeling consume him, he no longer worried about any darkness. His gaze fixed on Jeremy's, and he slipped into the guy's thoughts, twisting them to his will. Jeremy's laughter tapered off into a strange quiet, his eyes losing their focus.

"Hey, everyone," Kaos chimed in, his voice dripping with false friendliness. "You know what would be absolutely hilarious? If Jeremy here treated us to a little song."

Confused glances were exchanged among the others, but the odd request seemed intriguing enough to keep their attention. Especially since it was Kaos who was speaking. Jeremy, looking terrified, opened his mouth, and to his own bewilderment, he launched into singing a childish nursery rhyme. Laughter erupted from the group, as well as from the people around them. Enjoying the laughter he was causing, he pushed it a little further and made Jeremy begin to dance to his own music. Surely, to everyone else, they would assume that Jeremy was dancing out of fear. Fear that Kaos or Trace would do something to him if he didn't. Or they were probably suspecting Jeremy lost some sort of bet. That Kaos had explained to him that his punishment for losing the bet would come at any time, when he was least expecting it.

Kaos watched with a sinister grin as the guy sang and danced, caught in Kaos's spell. The cafeteria was a spectacle of laughing and staring, and Kaos reveled in the chaos he had conjured. His laughter mingled with the uproar, his power a twisted form of entertainment.

But at the table where The Unlikely Defenders sat, a different scene played out. Kire's expression darkened as he exchanged a glance with Rose. Amberly had her arms crossed and was staring at Kaos. Trace's fingers had curled into fists beneath the table. His disapproval was obvious and annoying to Kaos. Usually, Trace loved this sort of thing. Once upon a time, Trace stood by Kaos's side, and they made fun of Jeremy together.

Amid the echoing laughter, their table was a displeased island.

Kaos laughed loudly despite it, the sound echoing through the cafeteria. He noticed their stares, their silent judgment, and he merely shrugged, as if to dismiss their opinions.

He knew he wasn't supposed to use his powers for ill intent, but what did they expect from him?

4

———

When lunch ended, the cafeteria buzz spilled into the bustling hallway. Kaos, being a hidden observer, slipped into a casual stroll behind the other quintets. Amid the chatter, he strained to capture their words.

"Hey, Kire," Trace's voice held a friendly undertone. "What were you about to say earlier?"

Kire's shoulders sagged. "Oh, yeah, just... my folks separated."

"Because of me?" Amberly asked incredulously.

Kire shrugged like the answer was yes, but he would rather not say.

Trace's voice softened. "Tough deal. But hey, I've been doin' the single-parent thing for ages. It's not too bad."

Amberly's voice was laced with bitterness and empathy. "Gerald is the literal *worst*."

Rose's fingers tightened around Kire's, her voice soothing. "We're here for you, Kire. Are you okay?"

Kaos hovered like a phantom, turning out whatever else it was Kire was saying because his gaze was suddenly fixed on the back of Amberly. Amberly, her blonde locks kissed by sunlight, walked by Kire's side. Her presence stirred his longing.

He regretted his recklessness. The missed chance with her was an ache in his stomach—one he couldn't numb. Her sweet laughter echoed in his mind, memories replaying in his head from the times they had spent together the past few weeks. The smile on her face that Kaos had placed there because he was the one who had cheered her up after her mother passed.

As the others moved forward, Kaos realized it clearly: the group, even without him, seemed complete.

No, he told himself, shaking the bad thought away. *They'd be nothing without me. They need me.*

He belonged in their group, inside and outside of being a Defender. That meant he had to fix things. He had to make them right with Amberly.

Yet, he felt doubt creeping in. Could he fix his relationship with Amberly? Was it too late?

His fists clenched.

As they neared the classroom, Kaos reassured himself that it was at least worth trying.

After school, he decided he'd make his way to Amberly's house.

THE SCHOOL DAY had wrapped up, and Kaos stopped by his home before going to Amberly's Aunt Lydia's house. He wanted to give her a bit of time before he showed up so that it wasn't looking like a stressful ambush when she saw him.

Then, feeling nervous, he drove his dad's car over, each turn of the wheel making his stomach dip further.

Parking the car, he stared at Lydia's small, quaint home, adrenaline coursing through him. Taking a deep breath, he got out of the car and knocked on the front door, the sound echoing in the quiet street.

After a moment, the door opened, revealing Amberly, her eyes widening in surprise.

"Kaos? What are you doing here?" she asked. "And what was with you today, huh?"

Kaos shifted his weight, meeting her gaze with a serious expression as she crossed her arms and didn't offer to let him come in.

"Hey, Amberly. Can we talk?" he asked.

Amberly's eyebrows knitted together. "Is everything okay? Did something happen with Yash?"

He gave a half-smile. "I'm not here to bring bad news," he assured her, nodding over her shoulder. "Can I come in?"

Amberly hesitated, glancing over behind her before turning her attention back to him. "I don't know, Kaos."

Kaos's heart started racing. "Amberly, I just want to apologize. I know you're... *aware* of it already, but I messed up. I shouldn't have interfered between you and Trace, especially not the way I did."

Amberly's expression shifted from surprise to hurt. "Wow, I can't believe you're actually admitting it. So Trace and I were right then. You purposefully made me think Trace didn't want to be there for me after my mom passed away. And you told Trace that I needed space when I didn't?"

Kaos nodded, his gaze dropping briefly before returning to hers. "Yeah, that's exactly it. I know it was wrong, and I'm sorry for it."

She shook her head, her voice tinged with exasperation. "You can't just play with people's emotions like that, Kaos. You hurt both of us."

Kaos nodded again. "I know." He licked his lips and spat the words out. "But look, Amberly—you and I are a better match. We both have that fire in us, that passion to be on top. You—you have to agree with me. Look at how great these past few weeks together have been. I've been there for you through it all, haven't I? I always will be, too."

"Yeah, but... Kaos, the reason you and I spent all that time together is because *you* made it that way. You *manipulated* it into being that way. You don't need your crown to control the lives of the people around you. You're a natural."

Kaos shook his head quickly, mentally panicking because this was not going the way he wanted. "I-I messed up, Amberly. I shouldn't have done what I did, and I know that. Yeah, I sort of forced you and Trace to stay away from each other. But I never forced you to like being alone with me. To enjoy spending time with me. To come to me when you were feeling sad or whenever you had a problem. That was you, Amberly. You have to feel something for me. I'm just saying that maybe, just maybe, you and I understand each other better."

Amberly's arms dropped to her sides, her expression a mix of skepticism and bewilderment. "This is all so messed up, Kaos. I—"

She cut herself off and stared into the distance, shaking her head slowly. When she looked back at him, she let out a sigh, her gaze softening.

"Just—come on in."

Kaos followed her inside, feeling relieved.

"I need some water. I'll be right back," Amberly said before disappearing into the kitchen, leaving him alone in the living room. He sank onto the sofa, taking in the unfamiliar surroundings.

Moments later, another knock sounded on the door, and he turned his head to see Amberly's aunt, Lydia, heading toward it.

She opened it wide and greeted the unexpected guest with a curious expression. "Um, whoa. Hi there. W-what do you want?"

The reply came from beyond Kaos's view, a voice that sounded serious and grim. "I need to speak with Amberly."

Kaos's curiosity was piqued, and he shifted on the sofa to see who had arrived. It turned out to be none other than Gerald, Kire and Amberly's father. His appearance sent a ripple of surprise through the room.

Lydia's demeanor was guarded, her tone becoming more defensive. "And just why do you think I'd let you do that?"

Amberly's voice floated from the kitchen, tinged with curiosity. "Who is it?"

Gerald's gaze settled on Lydia, his expression unreadable. "I need to talk to her."

Lydia's eyes flickered with uncertainty.

As Amberly rounded the corner, the surprise on her face was evident. Kaos couldn't help but notice that this seemed like an unusual visit, as if Gerald had never set foot in this house before.

Lydia tried to intervene, her voice tinged with caution. "I can handle this, Amberly."

But Amberly's curiosity got the better of her. Ignoring Lydia's plea, she went to the door, her gaze locked onto her father's. "What do you want, *Dad*?"

Kaos watched the interaction unfold, deciding to stand up from the couch. His senses were heightened. He wanted to be ready in case he needed to intervene quickly should the situation escalate. He didn't have his crown because he wanted Amberly to know he had come in peace. But he badly wished he had decided to keep it on him.

The man on the doorstep appeared far from the menacing figure he'd been told about from Kire and Amberly. Instead, Gerald resembled a defeated shadow of himself. He remembered what Kire said earlier in the hallway. That his parents had separated. Did that have something to do with why Gerald was here now?

Gerald's voice trembled, filled with what might have been remorse. "Amberly, I'm—I'm sorry. I should've been there, but I wasn't. I ignored you, and I realize now how wrong that was."

Amberly appeared to be struggling internally, her eyes glistening as she fought back tears. The sight tugged at Kaos, the raw vulnerability in her expression showing a side he hadn't often seen. Amberly was revealing a layer of pain beneath her sassy demeanor. She didn't utter a word in response, not for a long minute.

But then, the biting edge in her voice was back, and she scoffed at Gerald's words. "Oh, how touching. The prodigal father returns with an apology."

Lydia's disdain was evident as well as she came to Amberly's aid. "Save the theatrics, Gerald. Amberly doesn't need to hear this from you."

Gerald's gaze shifted toward Lydia, a plea for understanding in his eyes. "Please, let me speak to Amberly alone. Just for a minute."

Lydia's response was venomous. "Yeah, because Amberly's been just *dying* to hear your voice."

"You're only here because your marriage is falling apart, right?" Amberly asked as she stood beside her aunt. "You're trying to save your own skin."

Gerald shot her an exasperated look. "Amberly, that's not true. I-I mean, *yes*, my marriage is in trouble, but it's made me realize how much I've messed up with you."

"Oh, *wonderful*," Amberly snapped. "You actually think I'm an idiot."

"Seriously. Don't think that we are buying it. That we could actually ever believe that this is the dawn of a new Gerald." Lydia put her arm around Amberly protectively.

Gerald's voice wavered. Kaos noticed that his expression lacked any warmth. He wasn't used to having to grovel. To force out apologies he didn't want to make. Kaos was on the side of Amberly and Lydia—Gerald was full of it. "Amberly, I'm *trying* to make amends. I know I've been a terrible father, but I want to change that. Can't you just hear me out?"

Amberly's gaze remained fixed on her father, her voice cutting. "You had *years* to be a father to me. It's a bit late for your redemption arc. Just leave me alone. Your monetary acknowledgment of my existence is more than enough."

Amberly turned away, her steps heavy with resentment as she retreated out of the room and into the hall. Kaos followed her, the two leaving Lydia and Gerald behind. As they headed toward her bedroom, the tension of the encounter still hung in the air, and

Kaos felt the need to take care of Amberly and make sure she was all right.

As he followed Amberly, he strained to catch the fading conversation between Lydia and Gerald.

"You heard the girl, Gerald. It's time for you to go. Don't come back."

The sound of the door slamming shut reverberated in Kaos's ears.

5

Later in the day, back at Kaos's house, his phone chimed, pulling his attention from his thoughts. He glanced at the screen, finding a message from Rose.

> Rose: Unlikely Defenders meeting @ Aunt Marg's.
> Be there.

The message quickly filled Kaos with anticipation. He practically lunged out of his bed, grabbed the car keys as quickly as possible, and dashed outside to his father's car.

As he drove, memories of his conversation with Amberly earlier, after her father had left, played like a movie in his mind. The heaviness in her voice, the way she held back tears—Kaos couldn't help but wish he was still alone with her, giving her the comfort that she needed. He recalled how he'd tried to console her, offering a shoulder to lean on as her emotions spilled forth. It was a side of Amberly that Kaos truly felt he was the only one to see it. Her vulnerability was reserved only to be exposed to him.

"I can't believe he had the audacity to show up like that," Amberly told Kaos as the two sat in her bedroom. Kaos understood her anger. Gerald's unexpected visit had brought back a flood of painful

memories and unresolved emotions for her. Add in Kaos trying to convince her to be with him instead of Trace. It was a lot for Amberly to handle in one day.

"I know it's complicated, Amberly," he'd offered, moving a little closer to her so that their knees were touching. "I don't know. Do you think maybe Gerald really wants to change? Because if you ask me, he just wants his wife back and doesn't care about anything else."

The tears continued down Amberly's face as she rested her head on his shoulder and stayed silent. Kaos rubbed her back in small circles of comfort. It had been an intimate moment, a connection he hadn't anticipated but cherished.

Now, as Kaos drove, Amberly's tear-streaked face haunted him, a reminder of the complexities lurking beneath her surface. He couldn't deny the satisfaction he'd felt when she'd leaned into his support; it felt like a step in the right direction of her choosing him. Leaving her house had left him with a renewed sense of hope, a belief that they could repair the damage that had been done between them, but also maybe more than that.

Turning into Aunt Marg's parking lot, Kaos's thoughts shifted to the present. He parked his car and took a moment to collect himself.

Then he stepped out of his dad's car, the setting sun reflecting off the polished surface. Adjusting the bright crown on his head—he put it back on as soon as he got home from Amberly's--he made his way toward the restaurant, which served as a quiet haven for The Unlikely Defenders. The establishment, nestled between the busy streets, was often where the group liked to come and strategize.

Pushing open the door, the comforting aroma of freshly baked goods enveloped him. The familiar scent was soothing. Kaos walked further inside, heading to the back room where they often held their private meetings. The room was a haven adorned with frilly tablecloths and delicate decor, and even though Kaos felt ridiculous inside of it at first, he had come to love the place.

Sliding into a chair, Kaos let out a sigh, his gaze scanning the empty chairs around him. He'd arrived early.

Impatient fingers tapped on the tabletop, and Kaos wondered how soon it would be before Trace showed. If Trace was going to be ready to hear anything Kaos had to say about trying to steal his girl-friend. He could admit to himself that he was feeling pretty doubtful.

As the minutes stretched on, Kaos worried that maybe something had happened to the others. He checked his phone to see if there were any updates in their group chat. But none appeared.

Just as frustration began to gnaw at him, the door creaked open once more. Trace stepped inside, his eyes darkening the second they met Kaos's gaze. The flaming sword that was Trace's magical gift was stored away in its scabbard. But Kaos knew he could pull it out at a moment's notice. He wondered what would happen if Trace tried to use the sword on him. They weren't supposed to be able to use their gifts on each other. But how would the magic prevent Trace from slicing Kaos's head right off the second he heard any of his excuses for what he did?

They exchanged a tense nod, the both of them remaining silent.

Kaos's heart raced in his chest as Trace took a seat across from him.

"Finally, one of you made it," Kaos remarked, his voice tinged with annoyance even though he didn't want it to come out that way.

Trace's lips twitched into a half-smile, both frustration and amusement in his eyes. "Is poor little Kaos annoyed he can't use his stupid crown to see when the others are going to arrive?"

Kaos rolled his eyes. "Apparently, I don't need my crown to get inside people's heads." It was a nod to how Kaos had manipulated Trace into staying away from Amberly when she needed him.

Trace leaned back, his expression growing serious. "Talking

about Amberly and me, huh? Are you saying you want to acknowledge your screwup to me?"

Kaos's gaze dropped, the guilt gnawing at his gut. "I never intended for things to get so messed up," he admitted.

Trace's stare bore into him. "Are you kidding me? What did you expect to happen? For Amberly and me to go our separate ways, glad for the breakup? For us to then be completely okay once my ex-girlfriend started dating my best friend? You are delusional."

The silence between them stretched on as Kaos tried to think of how to best reply. He hated having these confrontations with Trace. He hated not feeling in control of the situation. Eventually, he opened his mouth to respond, but realization about why they were the only two in the room suddenly slammed into him. And when he looked at Trace, he could see that he knew it, too.

"Wait a minute," Kaos began, "you don't think..."

Trace's lips curved into a bitter smile. "That we've been set up?"

The absurdity of the situation made Kaos roll his eyes. "The others..."

"They planned this," Trace finished. "They have no intention of being here. They wanted us to talk. Or at least, Rose did."

For a moment, they both laughed, amused by Rose's attempt to fix things. For a moment, everything felt like it was back to normal. But when the laughter died down. Kaos knew it wasn't.

Kaos and Trace then sat there in silence. Neither of them wanted to be the first to break it, even though deep down, Kaos knew he had to. The unity of The Unlikely Defenders depended on it, especially now when their gifts needed to be at their strongest.

Trace's jaw eventually clenched in anger, and Kaos wondered what it was he was thinking about. Was he upset that Kaos still hadn't attempted to rectify the situation further? He fidgeted with the edge of the frilly tablecloth, his mind racing for the right words. But Kaos had never been good at apologies, and this time was no exception.

"Look, about Amberly..." Kaos finally managed to mutter, his voice hesitant and unsure. What was he supposed to say? That he was sorry he broke them up, but that Amberly belonged with him? How was that going to solve anything?

Yet, it was the truth. It was what Kaos really wanted to say. He wanted to say it, and he wanted things to be okay after he did it. But he knew it wasn't possible.

Trace's eyes flicked up; his anger unrelenting. "I get the feeling that you were just fine with messing everything up."

Kaos sighed, frustration building within him. "That's not true, Trace. I just... I didn't mean to grow feelings for Amberly. I didn't know I would start to feel for her in that way. It's not really like I could stop it from happening, you know?"

Trace's eyebrows shot up, incredulity replacing some of the anger. "Are you seriously trying to get me to understand and accept why you did it? Are you trying to make me think it's okay? Because you fell for Amberly when you didn't even mean to?"

Kaos's frustration mounted, his words coming out all wrong, a jumbled mess of emotions. "No, that's not what I'm trying to do." However, it sort of was. "I just... I don't know, Trace. I can't help but feel that Amberly and I make more sense than you and her do. You've changed a lot. But Amberly hasn't really changed that much. And neither have I. And these past few weeks, I've kept her safer than you ever have."

Kaos knew he had said the wrong thing immediately. He could see the fire in Trace's eyes. "*Safer*? You put your own selfish desires above our mission, our friendship!"

Before Kaos could respond, a sudden and powerful tremor seized the room, shaking everything within it.

Plates clinked, glasses rattled, and the frilly decorations swayed dangerously. The ground quaked beneath them, and Kaos instinctively reached out to grip the edge of the table for support.

"What the...?" Kaos's voice was lost amid the rumbling chaos.

Trace's eyes widened, his anger momentarily forgotten as he, too, struggled to maintain his balance. The force of the shaking was overpowering, the noise deafening. Kaos's heart raced as he exchanged a stunned glance with Trace, the realization dawning on both of them.

The tremors intensified, the room vibrating with otherworldly power. As the rumbling grew louder, it was as if the very foundations of the building were being tested. The restaurant's delicate decor swayed ominously, and Kaos's mind raced to find an explanation.

"An earthquake?" Trace yelled to Kaos.

Kaos shook his head, a sinking feeling gnawing at his gut. "I don't think so. It's something else."

As if on cue, the noise reached a deafening crescendo, drowning out everything else. The very air seemed to vibrate with a power that defied explanation. Kaos's mind raced, thoughts of Yash and the impending danger consuming him. This couldn't be a mere coincidence. Yash was coming, and they were unprepared, weakened by their own disagreement.

The realization hit Kaos like a bolt of lightning. He met Trace's eyes, the fear mirrored in his friend's gaze. Their argument, their weakened abilities—it was all a mistake they couldn't afford to make.

"If it's Yash, Halo would have said something!" Trace yelled.

"Yeah, but Kire isn't here!"

As the rumbling finally subsided, leaving behind an eerie silence, Kaos and Trace shared a scared look. Without a word, Kaos pushed himself to his feet.

"We need to find the others," Kaos said, his voice steady despite the tremors still rattling his bones.

Trace nodded. "Yeah, you're right."

With Kaos giving the place a last look, they left behind the shaken room, their footsteps pounding the cracked pavement as they bolted out of the restaurant quickly and urgently. Outside, they were met with a scene of chaos. People were emerging from nearby buildings, their faces confused and scared. But what caught *Kaos's* attention was the group of other Defenders, standing just a few feet away in the parking lot, talking worriedly to one another.

Amberly, Rose, and Kire stood there, looking shaken and concerned. As Kaos and Trace joined them, they shared a moment of shared understanding.

"Is it Yash?" Kaos asked. "Did Halo tell you?" He ignored the fact that the others had been here the whole time, waiting for Trace and him to resolve their fight. He wondered when Amberly appeared. When Rose and Kire told her their idea.

"Halo hasn't said anything," Kire replied, his face pale.

Without exchanging words, the group set off in the direction of a growing commotion on the street. A crowd of people had gathered at a distance, their whispers growing louder as they exchanged worried glances.

The five teens pushed through the gathering until they stood at the edge of a massive sinkhole that had appeared out of thin air. It was a breathtaking sight—a rift of unimaginable proportions, nearly a quarter of a mile wide in diameter, opening up like a bad bullet wound in the surface of the earth.

Kaos's heart pounded as he stared at the abyss, his mind struggling to comprehend the scale of the devastation before him. How had this happened? Was it a mere coincidence? A natural phenomenon?

Or was it something else?

Amberly's voice trembled as she spoke, the disbelief evident in her words. "What... what could have caused this?"

The townspeople around them murmured and talked worriedly among themselves, sharing theories and speculations. But The Unlikely Defenders exchanged the same concerned glances for other reasons no one else knew. Kaos could tell the others were wondering the same thing. That maybe this wasn't a natural disaster. Maybe it was a sign of something far more sinister. Yash—the powerful being they dreaded—could potentially be beginning his assault on their world.

Kaos's looked at the others seriously. And they all looked back at him, ready for his guidance. He knew that the time for disagreements and personal conflicts was over. The Unlikely Defenders needed to unite like never before, to harness their individual gifts and stand together against the impending threat.

"We need to find out more about what's happening," Rose said, her voice laced with urgency.

Kire nodded in agreement. "We can't let this sinkhole be the first of many."

Trace's jaw clenched as he looked at the chasm before them. "So, it really was Yash?"

"The coincidence would be too huge," Amberly said. "Maybe he hasn't started complete destruction yet, and that is why Halo hasn't warned us. But still, we can't waste any more time."

As the townspeople continued to speculate and fret, The Unlikely Defenders exchanged one last determined look. They were all that stood between Yash and the world's destruction.

6

Kaos stood at the edge of the massive sinkhole that had suddenly appeared in the heart of Montgomery. His eyes were wide, his heart pounding. Beside him, Kire, Amberly, Trace, and Rose shared his shock and worry. The small town they'd grown up in was now a scene of chaos and devastation.

Cars had fallen into the gaping hole in the ground, and flames licked at the edges of buildings that teetered on the brink while others lay in ruins. People stumbled through the debris, some with bloodied faces, their voices a cacophony of panic. Sirens wailed in the distance, mixing with the blaring horns of vehicles that had been caught in the chaos.

"I think it's time we keep planning," Kaos told the others.

Kire shook his head as he stared down at the crater, a huge portion of the town down inside of it. He was still in disbelief. Kaos wondered if his head was stuck like that, in a shaking motion. "I've never seen anything like this."

Amberly trembled as she stared into it as well. Kaos watched as Trace stepped closer to her. It didn't feel good to see. "Sinkholes just don't appear out of nowhere, do they?" She asked if the others.

"What is everyone going to think? What if they start speculating that something... otherworldly possibly caused this to happen?"

Trace's eyes were wide, scanning the wreckage around them. "Look at *that*," he pointed at a twisted lamp post bent at an odd angle. "It's like something burst out of the ground."

This caused Rose to grow horrified. She looked at Trace, quivering. "You mean, you think maybe something *came* out of that hole? Something... relatively the same size of it?"

Kaos hadn't considered the possibility that Yash was massive. As massive as this hole in the ground. But would that be really how he arrived on Earth? Through the center of it? It didn't seem likely. Kaos was certain that Yash's arrival would come from above, in the sky.

"I know we need to keep planning," Kire piped up. "But... we need to help those people, shouldn't we? I mean... look at them. They're hurt and scared."

As they watched, firefighters worked frantically to put out the fires, police officers tried to manage the chaos, and paramedics attended to the injured. The town that had always seemed so peaceful was now a battleground of destruction.

Kaos's thoughts raced. The image of it all would not be erased from his memory anytime soon. Maybe even ever. "The firefighters and paramedics have a handle on it," he decided.

Kire frowned, his brow furrowing. Kaos could tell what he was thinking. Kire felt as though this was all their fault. They had killed Rezin, and now other people were hurt.

"First the fire, now this," Trace said, his eyes glazed over. Guilt appeared to be consuming him. "This... this is on a whole different level. It's like the earth itself is tearing apart."

Kaos nodded slowly. "How are we going to fix it?"

Their eyes met.

"How are we going to stop Yash?" Amberly added. She looked highly doubtful that it was even possible.

Beside her, Kire clenched his fists, his expression hardened. "We will think of something. We... we can't let him succeed."

Trace scratched his head, looking uncertain about something. Then he said, "My house is closest. I know that I don't typically have people over, but... I think I can make an exception. For this. I say we go there and figure out what the heck we're going to do."

Nods of agreement followed, and Kaos felt relieved as the group began to move. They would fix this. One way or another. They had to.

Trace's house quickly appeared in the distance, a modest structure in a dilapidated neighborhood. While it was relatively close to the sinkhole, it looked unaffected by the terrifying event. As they entered his home, the sense of familiarity enveloped Kaos. The aroma of Trace's mom's cooking, the worn-out couch they'd spent countless hours on, the familiar pictures on the wall—everything was as it should be, and yet everything was utterly wrong.

Vivian, Trace's mother, was seated on the couch, her eyes locked onto the television screen. The news was on, the anchor's voice loud and serious. The sinkhole, the fires, the destruction—it was all being broadcasted into the living room, a grim reminder of the world outside.

"Mom, how are you doing?" Trace's voice was gentle, as if his tone was trying to offer reassurance.

Vivian jumped at the sound of her son, her eyes wide with fear.

"Oh, Trace! You're safe." She reached out, gripping her son's arm as if to confirm his presence.

Trace gave her a weak smile, likely trying to mask his concern. "Yeah, Mom, we're all safe."

Vivian looked at the others, her gaze lingering on each face as if memorizing their features. "You kids... did you see it? Were you outside when it happened? It's dangerous out there. Much too dangerous for you all. Stay inside. We don't know what caused the sinkhole or if there are going to be others."

Amberly stepped forward, her voice friendly and calming. "Hi, Vivian. It's nice to see you again."

"Amberly," Vivian said, reaching an arm out and covering the side of Amberly's face gently, giving her a warm smile. "I'm so sorry about your mother."

"Mom," Trace interrupted. "Now is not the time."

Vivian turned back to Trace and grabbed his arm again, her grip tighter this time.

"Promise me you'll be careful," she told him before turning to the others. "Promise me you won't let anything happen to my boy."

"Relax, Mom," Trace said. "We're fine. I'm fine. It's just a sinkhole."

Kaos's stomach dipped. He knew it was more than that.

With a final, lingering look, Vivian sighed heavily and started to walk away from the living room. "I think I need a nap," she told the others as she left.

Kaos's heart ached. This was a world-changing event, one that could quite literally tear everything apart.

He turned to Trace and Amberly, his two closest friends who had become entangled in a web of complicated problems. He felt heavy with regret about the choices he had made. He was the sinkhole in their trio. If the world was about to end, did he want it to end with their relationship like this?

He cleared his throat and clapped his hands together. "All right." His voice was firm, his eyes meeting theirs, determined. "We need to figure out how to stop this. We're the only ones who can do it."

Trace nodded, his muscles tensed. "We'll need to gather information and see if we can find any clues about what's really going on."

Amberly looked at Kire's backpack. "If only we could use Halo."

"Hey," Kire interrupted. "Consider it a good thing that we haven't heard from Halo. That only means that Yash isn't officially here yet. We would have been warned otherwise."

His words made Amberly look a little calmer. It also made Kaos feel a little better. Kire had to be right. Halo wouldn't lie to them, right?

Time slipped by, their focus solely on the task at hand.

Yet, their strategizing was abruptly interrupted an hour later when Vivian reappeared from her room, her demeanor drastically altered.

Trace's eyes widened as he took in his mother's disheveled appearance—swaying unsteadily, bloodshot eyes, slurred speech.

Anger flashed across his face, a huge contrast to the concern he had shown earlier. "No way—*Mom*," he growled. "Are you... kidding me?"

Vivian's shoulders slumped, her voice barely coherent. "Trace, I... I had *a* drink, okay? Just one. I needed something to calm my nerves after... After all of this." She gestured vaguely toward the television, hiccuping slightly.

Trace's fists clenched at his sides, his jaw set. "*Unbelievable.* You can't even stay sober for a crisis like this? I thought you wanted to keep me safe. How are you supposed to do that when you're drunk?"

Again, Kaos had found himself in the middle of an awkward family confrontation. He knew Trace was going to be embarrassed about this; he didn't like anyone knowing about his mother's state.

Vivian's eyes filled with regret, her voice growing desperate. "I'm trying, Trace. You know it's not that simple."

Amberly exchanged a sympathetic glance with Kaos, her eyes full of questioning. Kaos knew she wasn't aware of a whole lot about Trace's mother. Embarrassed by the life he lived and not wanting to overshadow Amberly being in a similar situation with her own mother, he stayed silent about it for most of their relationship.

Then, probably because she wanted to help, Amberly stepped forward, her tone gentle. "Vivian, maybe we can—"

Trace's voice was sharp, his frustration boiling over. "No, Amberly, you don't get it. You can't fix this. None of you can."

Kaos felt like an intruder in this intensely personal moment. He could see the struggle in Trace's eyes—the love he had for his mother battling against anger and disappointment. Kaos truly felt bad for his friend. He lost his girlfriend. His mother was sick and constantly drinking. And now, he also had the weight of having to save the world on his shoulders. It was a lot to deal with.

"Trace..." Amberly tried.

With a bitter laugh, Trace harshly yanked Kire's backpack from the floor. He ripped it open and pulled out the teleportation stone. "I'm done. I can't deal with any of this. I'm leaving, and I'm not coming back."

The gang followed Trace outside, the front door slamming shut behind them. The evening air was frigid and ominous, warning everyone that that sinkhole wasn't going to be the last.

Trace's voice carried through the night as he shouted his intentions to the others.

"I'm going to the Albus realm. I'll stay there forever. I'm *not* coming back to this messed-up world!"

Kaos exchanged helpless glances with Amberly, Kire, Rose, and even Trace. They were powerless in the face of Trace's anger, unable to find the right words to convince him otherwise. Kaos cast a final curious glance over his shoulder through the window into the living room of Trace's house, catching a glimpse of Vivian slumping onto the couch with a heavy sigh.

7

"Guys, just wait a second!" Kaos yelled to the others who were trying to chase after Trace, who was fleeing from them. Upon Kaos's command, they all stopped and turned back to him. He beckoned them over, and they gathered in Trace's front yard, each one of them looking deeply concerned about the fifth member of The Unlikely Defenders.

Kaos knew Trace well. He understood that Trace needed a moment, that he wanted to be alone. Chasing after him wasn't going to solve anything.

"What?" Amberly snapped at Kaos, glancing over her shoulder to see if Trace was still in sight. He was, but it didn't matter if they lost sight of him.

"He's going to the Albus realm," Kaos pointed out calmly. "We don't need to chase him. We know where to find him."

"But he's saying he's not going to come back!" Amberly cried. "His mom..."

Kaos nodded somberly.

"Why didn't you ever say anything?" Amberly asked, her voice quivering.

"I didn't realize it was my job to tell you about your own

boyfriend's life problems," Kaos retorted, a tinge of frustration in his tone.

"Amberly?" Rose interjected, placing trembling fingers to her mouth. "You mean... you didn't know about his mom?"

"Did *you*?" Amberly shot back.

Rose stayed silent at that.

"*Ugh!*" Amberly stomped her feet. "What the heck are we supposed to *do*, Kaos? What's your big genius plan? Because he's talking about not coming back ever!"

"Yeah, and, Kaos, the Albus realm isn't exactly small," Kire added. "We know Trace is going there, but what about after? He has the stone."

"Fine," Kaos conceded. "We'll follow him, but we'll stay far enough back until we get to the portion of the cave with the portal. I don't want him to know we're following."

The others nodded in agreement, no one questioning why Kaos wanted them to remain hidden. Perhaps it was evident to everyone that Kaos's approach was their best chance to reach Trace, given his deep connection with their troubled friend. Nobody wanted to escalate the situation further.

Together, they jogged until they reached the forest and spotted Trace just up ahead. They slowed to a crawl, ducking behind trees and taking care to muffle the sound of their footsteps on the leaves.

Slowly but surely, with Rose's assistance, around them, The White Forest was recovering from the fire that Trace had ignited. It was just too bad that *another* disaster now plagued the town.

There were a few moments when Trace glanced over his shoulder, likely hearing the occasional twig snap under their feet. Each time he did, they all hunkered down.

"This is stupid," Amberly hissed, prompting a sharp, "Shush!" from Rose.

Trace turned around again, but he continued on his path, undeterred.

By the time they reached the cave, maintaining complete

silence had become impossible. The cave's acoustics were unforgiving, and their footsteps and even their hushed breaths reverberated loudly.

"I know you're back there," Trace growled from somewhere ahead. He didn't use any light sources, so while they could hear his voice, they couldn't see him.

Kaos wondered if Trace intended to try to lose them, taking a different route or perhaps finding a shadowed alcove to hide and wait for them to pass into the Albus realm, only to find Trace had remained in the Earth realm.

Rose became their source of light since Trace wasn't using his sword. She summoned not only lightning bugs, but also bioluminescence that shimmered along the cave walls, providing ample illumination.

"Trace, can't we just talk about this?" Amberly called out, turning her head sharply to the others afterward. "We might as well blow our cover; he said himself that he knows we're back here," she snapped defensively, even though none of them had criticized her for calling out to Trace in the first place. It was as though she expected a response from them and had already prepared her rebuttal.

"Leave me alone," Trace called out. "All of you."

"Why don't you just *talk* to us?" Amberly called again after him.

"It's not a big deal," Kaos added. "To *us*, I mean. We don't think any differently of you after seeing Vivian like that. Come on. It's us."

"Like *that's* saying much," Trace retorted, taking a jab at Kaos and Amberly's previous betrayal.

Amberly hit Kaos on the arm with the back of her hand, but he hardly reacted; he was used to Amberly's harmless, bossy swats. "We need to fix this," she whispered urgently.

Kaos nodded. "Let's just follow him from back here, and when he's ready to talk... we'll talk."

"*That's* your plan?" Amberly growled. "What if he *never* wants to talk? We can't stay in the Albus realm forever, not with no idea what's happening here."

"When we get back, I bet you only minutes will have passed. Just chill."

Amberly took a slow, deep breath, and they all fell silent, trailing behind Trace until they reached the archway at the bottom of the drained lake along their hidden path in the cave. One by one, they closed their eyes and stepped through the swirling blue arch. When they opened their eyes again, they found themselves in the Albus realm.

The day was gorgeous, with birds chirping, the sun shining brightly, and white fluffy clouds lazily drifting across the sky.

But Trace remained a storm.

"If you're going to use the stone, at least take us with you," Kire called to Trace, who had halted in the cornfield on the hill, as if contemplating where to go and what to do.

"I'm going to see Novus," Trace responded.

Kaos watched Amberly closely, anticipating her reaction. Her face stiffened, but she swallowed her emotions and approached Trace.

"Then *we're* going to see Novus."

"And I'm *staying* there," Trace reminded them.

"You don't belong here, Trace. None of us do," Rose tried. No one else replied as they placed their hands on the rock and were transported to a location inside the magical realm.

They landed in the village where Novus resided, right in the middle of the town square, in front of the water well. Kaos hardly felt dizzy this time, wondering if he was getting accustomed to the sensation of teleportation.

Trace's expression remained dark as he glanced at them and then turned sharply, stalking off once more.

"Maybe he needs to talk to Novus," Rose suggested. "As an outsider who didn't witness the situation with his mom, she might be the one who can calm him down better."

"Doubtful," Amberly said, crossing her arms.

They followed Trace from a distance all the way to Novus's quaint cottage, which looked like it came straight out of a fairytale book. Chickens roamed the front yard, windows were open, and smoke billowed from the chimney. Birds sang harmoniously, and the scent of something delicious cooking filled the air.

"Why don't you guys just stay out here since you insist on following me?" Trace asked before approaching Novus's front door.

"Fat chance of that happening," Amberly snapped, moving past him and knocking on the door herself, harder than necessary.

Kaos couldn't help but feel a twinge of unease at how bothered Amberly was by Trace seeking the attention of another girl, but he pushed those thoughts aside. None of it mattered right now.

Novus answered the door, and her lips curved into a small smile. "Trace?" she asked, glancing at him and then the others. "What are you all doing here?"

Novus Applerose was half-human, half-fairy. She had vibrant red hair and a shimmering iridescent cloak around a pink dress. It was clear Amberly saw her as a threat because Novus was definitely striking to look at, so Kaos thought. When she stepped into the sunlight, everything about her had an ethereal glow. Her hair, her eyes, even her skin brightened and shimmered.

"Noelle, *hi*," Amberly greeted in a feigned cheerful tone, purposefully forgetting her name.

"Amberly, come on," Trace grumbled.

Novus's smile remained undiminished. "It's all right, Trace," she replied with a nod of respect. "Hello, Amberly." She stepped aside to allow everyone to enter her small cottage. "So, the last time you were here to retrieve those artifacts and confront Yash's servant, how did it go?"

"Not as we expected," Trace answered preemptively. "But I don't want to dive into that right now. I actually came to talk to you about something important."

"Trace, think about what you're about to say," Rose interjected from behind Kaos, making her presence known.

"What is it?" Novus asked, her gaze shifting between Trace and Rose.

"We aren't entirely certain that the sinkhole was even caused by Yash," Rose continued. "It seems likely, but still..."

"You're only making it easier for me not to go back," Trace cut her off.

"What do you mean?" Rose inquired.

"If the sinkhole really is just that—a sinkhole—then there's no rush for me to return. No pressure to join you and participate in the fight."

"Join them?" Novus raised a pale eyebrow. "What do you mean? Did you just say you want to stay here?"

Trace turned back to face her. "I... I do. That's what I wanted to talk to you about."

"Geez, Trace, are you already asking the girl if you can move in with her?" Kaos couldn't help but chuckle at the shocked expressions on everyone's faces as he posed the question.

"N-no," Trace stammered, briefly glaring at Kaos before returning his attention to the fairy woman. "Did you mean it when you said I'd fit in here? That I can make a decent living as a knight and find a good place to live?"

Novus radiated light as she replied, "Of course."

"Come on," Trace said to the others as he addressed Novus. "A freaking *knight*. Try and tell me that's not worth staying for."

"I know you care about what happens to the people in your own realm," Rose said, looking offended. She seemed just as hurt as if he were personally attacking her by not coming back.

"You can't just leave your mom like that, Trace," Amberly added. "She needs you."

"Is your mother all right?" Novus asked, gently placing a hand on Trace's shoulder.

"She's fine. Or she'll have to be. One way or another, she's gonna have to figure it out on her own because I'm done."

"Did something happen?"

"Guys," Kire suddenly interjected, his gaze fixed outside the window. "We've got company."

A group of townspeople was approaching Novus's cottage. Kaos would typically be on high alert at the sight of such a gathering, but they all seemed to be in good spirits. They had relaxed postures, and none of them were wielding torches and pitchforks—a good sign.

Novus opened her door once more and welcomed them with a smile.

"Some people mentioned they saw you lot in the town square not long ago," the head of the group, a middle-aged man with his hands on his hips and his chest jutting out proudly, called. He and about twelve others had come to say hello.

"The Unlikely Defenders are here, you're correct!" Novus cried, ushering the teenagers as if they were a famous band and she was their manager, forcing them to sign autographs. These people weren't seeking autographs, though; they simply wanted to be near The Unlikely Defenders, to talk to them, maybe get some assistance with repairs, and to learn about the ongoing struggle with Yash.

"Hello," Rose greeted everyone, her voice slightly shaky. She looked nervous but determined. Kaos was surprised to see her addressing such a large crowd—when had Rose become comfortable speaking to large audiences? "I was wondering if any of you could convince Trace that he doesn't belong in this realm," she implored. "The only way we'll be strong enough to fight Yash is if he comes back to the Earth realm with us and helps us prepare for battle. We need to train and strategize, and we can't do it without him, but he's insisting on staying here."

"There's going to be a battle?" the group's leader inquired. The others began murmuring among themselves, their tones indecipherable.

"Probably the biggest one yet," Kire affirmed. "Yes, Yash wants to destroy our realm. He might already be causing chaos while we're here." He cast a bitter look at Trace.

"No one asked you guys to come with me," Trace jeered.

"Well, hold on a second," a young man interjected, pushing his way through the crowd. He appeared to be in his early twenties. "If you're gearing up for battle, surely you'll need an army."

For a moment, The Unlikely Defenders exchanged glances.

"What, you'd come *help* us?" Amberly asked, her voice breathless.

"The portal is open, isn't it?" another person chimed in. "We could go back with you when it's time to fight."

"You just say the word," added someone else.

"This is perfect," Kaos muttered to the others. "We need all the help we can get."

"They'd be risking their lives," Rose whispered to Kaos and Kire.

"I don't know if I could live with myself if anyone died," Kire added.

"Look, none of us can hear what you're saying from over here," the group's leader called out. "Why don't you fill us in on what's happened so far? Let us help in any way we can. It's the least we can do. You protected our realm from Yash's faithful servants. And you helped us rebuild."

"See? You don't have to feel guilty," Kaos whispered to Rose and Kire. "They're returning the favor."

Kaos stepped forward and gave everyone a quick wave before launching into an explanation of everything that had transpired in the Earth realm. He described the sinkhole in Montgomery and their strong suspicion that it was caused by Yash.

"I wouldn't be here then if I were you," one of the townspeople commented. "What if the situation is worsening while you're here with us?"

"Just a minor... hiccup we have to deal with," Kaos assured them.

"He's right," Trace agreed, not referring to Kaos but to the other townsfolk. "You guys shouldn't be here. You need to investigate the sinkhole further and determine if there are any traces of something otherworldly, magical, or alien. Or if it just appears to be a regular old sinkhole."

"Then come with us," Amberly implored.

"No."

She stomped her foot in frustration. "Trace!"

"Come on, bro," Kaos urged.

Once again, Trace shot Kaos a dirty look. "We're not bros, *bro*."

Ouch.

"Well, we can stay here arguing about this all day while our world's getting destroyed by the sinkhole, or we can let Trace pout here, check on the sinkhole, and figure out what to do next once we know what the situation is," Kire proposed. It was the only plan that made sense, the one they could all agree upon. Kaos understood Trace's stubbornness all too well and knew that trying to persuade him any longer wouldn't benefit anyone.

For now, Trace was staying.

8

Kaos couldn't help but feel like a celebrity among the inhabitants of the Albus realm. To them, The Unlikely Defenders weren't just protectors of Earth; they were guardians of multiple realms, and that certainly felt like hero status. They couldn't even head straight back to the portal after deciding to return to the sinkhole because the townspeople wanted to engage with them. They sought their opinions, offered advice, and some even insisted on sharing their homemade treats.

As the group approached the edge of town, Novus walked with everyone, including Trace. However, Kaos noticed that Trace stood back, arms crossed, beside Novus, not participating in the farewell waves.

"Are you seriously going to stay?" Amberly asked, mirroring Trace's body language.

"I'll make sure he's well taken care of," Novus responded on Trace's behalf, which clearly didn't sit well with Amberly, judging by her expression.

"Amberly, if Trace wants to stay, just let him," Kaos chimed in, offering his perspective. He wanted to tell her to stop being jealous and to see what was right in front of her, but he kept those feelings to himself, as he often did.

"Oh, before you go!" Novus called out, her eyes fixing on Rose. "Rose, do you mind if I have a chat with you for a moment?"

Rose sounded a bit caught off guard but excited as she responded, "Oh." Kaos had noticed Rose's fascination with Novus from the moment they had first met.

Rose let go of Kire's hand, and the two of them, who seemed inseparable lately, watched as Rose and Novus walked away from the crowd, leaving Trace behind.

Kaos couldn't help but wonder what private conversation Novus needed to have with Rose. As far as he knew, Rose had only encountered Novus once when Trace had brought them to her cottage to seek help on how to defeat Rezin.

So, what could Novus want from Rose now?

Kaos didn't have much time to dwell on this, as it became clear that their teleportation with the stone would be further delayed. One of their devoted fans, a younger guy in the group, started bombarding Trace with enthusiastic questions about swordsmanship and his potential usefulness in battles across realms. Kaos found it difficult to get a word in edgewise, and just when he thought the interrogation would never end, Rose suddenly returned.

"Are we ready to go?" she asked, casting a pleasant glance at everyone.

"Yep," Amberly replied, snatching the stone out of Trace's hand with one final glare. They exchanged goodbyes one last time, even Trace joining in with a small wave.

"Stay safe," Kaos told Trace, nodding at his old friend.

"Yeah..." Trace trailed off briefly. "Whatever."

And with that, the four Unlikely Defenders left the fifth Defender behind.

THE FOLLOWING MORNING, Kaos mentioned that he still had school, even though the town was in a state of panic due to the sudden appearance of the sinkhole. His parents grew furious and started making phone calls.

I didn't even use my crown for that one, he thought to himself, wondering why his parents even cared about his school attendance when they were still planning to go to work. It wasn't as if they were going to stay home to take care of him.

In the end, his parents couldn't get the school shut down for the day. Kaos didn't want to miss an English test, even though school should have been the last thing on his mind at a time like this. Halo hadn't informed them that Yash was coming, and in the unlikely event that they defeated him and their world survived, Kaos still had college to think about.

Arriving at school after picking up the others, two of them missing, Kaos noticed that Amberly was in a terrible mood, snapping at everyone as soon as she got into the car.

"Is this because Trace isn't here?" Kire asked while Kaos checked his phone and then continued driving. Kaos couldn't quite tell if Kire was being snooty toward Amberly or sincere.

"This has *nothing* to do with him," Amberly sneered. "I just... I didn't sleep well. That's why I'm being grouchy. Sorry."

"Has anyone heard from Rose this morning?" Kaos inquired, unsure whether he should try to go to her house, as she wasn't responding to the group chat.

"Kire?" Amberly bit out. "*You're* the boyfriend. Why isn't she responding?"

"I don't know," Kire replied. "I haven't talked to her since last night."

"Well, I'm not going to bother picking her up then. She'll have to find her own way to school," Kaos decided, driving toward the school. It felt strange with just the three of them—no Trace, no Rose.

"I just hope everything's okay with her," Kire sighed as Kaos pulled into his elite parking spot in the student lot. Kaos adjusted the crown on his head, not feeling ready for the English test. But readiness didn't matter; as long as he could manipulate his teacher, he'd secure an A on the test, no reading or studying required.

"Heaven forbid you're separated from the love of your life for a *single* day," Amberly quipped to Kire, rolling her eyes as they all climbed from the car. "She's fine, Kire. Don't be such a worrywart."

She stormed ahead of the two of them as the bell signaled it was time for their first class.

"She's definitely moody because of Trace. I don't care *what* she says," Kire confided in Kaos.

"*Dude*," Kaos replied, shaking his head. Kire should have known he was the last person who would want to discuss Amberly and Trace's relationship.

Rather than walking alongside Kire any longer, Kaos caught up to Amberly.

"Forget about him," he urged to her, talking about Trace. "He's being a baby. He left you behind, Amberly, to hang out with some other girl. Doesn't that bother you?"

"Duh," she snapped.

"Then why are you so upset about him not being here? He doesn't want to be here, so just forget about him."

"You don't get it, Kaos," she said, pausing in her step once they entered the school and looking down at the floor. Bodies moved around them, including Kire's, and for a moment, Kaos could've sworn Amberly was about to burst into tears.

"I just..." she started.

"What is it?" Kaos asked, offering a comforting hand on her arm. She stared at it for a while, saying nothing.

"I can't do this right now, okay?" She removed his hand, gave him a small headshake, and disappeared into the throng of students.

. . .

Kaos searched for Rose in their shared classes and even during lunch, but it was evident she wouldn't be attending school that day.

"I'm really starting to get freaked out," Kire admitted, approaching Kaos in the hallway between classes as the school day neared its end. "It's not like her to go this long without saying something to me."

"What do you think might've happened?" Kaos inquired.

Kire looked around to ensure no one was eavesdropping before speaking in a hushed voice that barely cut through the hallway noise. "Do you remember in the Albus realm when Rose was talking to Novus?"

Kaos had completely forgotten about it until that moment. "Yeah?" he replied to Kire's inquiry.

"Well... Do you remember the deal we made with Novus?"

"Money for the artifacts in exchange for a favor," Kaos recalled. "Do you think Rose has gone off somewhere to fulfill a favor for Novus, then?"

Kire shrugged. "I don't know. It's the only thing that makes sense."

"Do you think she went to the sinkhole without us?" Kaos asked again.

"N-not until you just said that!" Kire replied, his eyes wide with alarm.

Kaos gripped Kire's shoulders and gave him a small shake. "Keep it together," he instructed. "School's almost out for the day. Then we'll go look at the sinkhole. I've been keeping my eye on the news, checking my phone every hour. The sinkhole hasn't gotten any worse. No new ones are popping up in other parts of the country. And you haven't heard from Halo, right?"

"Right."

"Okay."

The two nodded at each other before parting ways. However, when the school day ended, Kire didn't seem any less freaked out and worried, while Amberly still appeared as though she might never smile again. Kaos briefed her on the plan and shared the discussion he had with Kire in the hallway about Rose.

"If she doesn't show up at the sinkhole," he said, sending a text in the group chat for Rose to see about meeting them there, "then I think it'll be safe to say that something isn't right."

"Something is *already* not right," Kire mumbled.

"*Nothing* is right," Amberly added.

"Okay, drama queens," Kaos snapped. "Are we ready to go to the sinkhole or not?"

Kire and Amberly exchanged glances, both appearing utterly miserable.

"Geez," Kaos commented dryly. "You two are *definitely* related."

"Shut up," Amberly muttered. "Let's just get this over with."

9

etting close to the sinkhole presented quite a challenge. Not only were news vans still scattered everywhere, but the area was also cordoned off with caution tape, with curious onlookers trying to catch a glimpse from behind the barriers. The fires it had ignited had been extinguished, and tow trucks stationed around the perimeter had managed to extract only a handful of cars from the wreckage. The rest lay concealed deep within the colossal crater. If Kaos didn't know better, he might have mistaken it for a meteor that had crash-landed during the night.

The sheer enormity of the hole was staggering, and even the news reports seemed to echo the disbelief surrounding this disaster.

No one else will ever know it, Kaos mused to himself as they approached the taped-off site, *but this isn't a natural or geological catastrophe.* He couldn't shake the feeling that Yash was responsible for the sinkhole's creation. It would be too much of a coincidence otherwise.

"What exactly are we looking for?" Kire inquired, his furrowed brow showing that he was still irritated and concerned about the Rose situation. Kaos sensed that he would rather be searching for his girlfriend than investigating the sinkhole. Nevertheless, their duty to protect their realm was far more important than locating one single specific missing person.

Especially one who's scared of harmless animals and obsessed with plants, Kaos thought, a faint smile tugging at his lips as he appreciated his own humor.

"You're just *loving* this, aren't you?" Amberly remarked, catching Kaos with a smile on his face.

"No," he hastily replied, wiping the smirk away. He hadn't meant for her to see that. "I just..." He stumbled for an excuse, coming up empty. "I'm not exactly sure what it is we're supposed to be looking for."

"Do you expect us to go *in* it?" Amberly inquired.

"Not gonna happen," Kire chimed in. "I don't feel like dying today, thank you very much."

"What if Rose fell in there?" she asked casually.

"Don't say that!" Kire snapped.

"Guys!" Kaos shouted at them. "Stop acting like a couple of whiny babies. Come on." They pushed their way through the crowd toward the sinkhole. Kaos tried to attune himself to the surroundings, seeking any sign the sinkhole might offer that hinted at Yash's involvement.

Reaching the tape blocking the area, Kaos put his mind-manipulating powers to the test. Despite two Unlikely Defenders missing from their group, he managed to utilize his gift effectively—a city employee lifted the tape and signaled for the three of them to pass underneath. When other onlookers began to complain about the apparent favoritism, the city worker responded in a monotone voice, "It's for a project for their science class," just as Kaos had intended.

"I can't believe that worked," Kaos said, satisfied with his manipulation.

"Me neither," Amberly agreed, her voice tinged with sadness. "Not without the other two." Her lip quivered. "*God, I feel so* stupid," she whispered to Kaos, turning so that only he could hear her, not Kire. "I kind of thought that Trace would've come to his senses by now and come back."

"Amberly..." Kaos trailed off, unsure of what else to say. Amberly looked devastated by Trace's decision to stay in the Albus realm with Novus. Bringing up the fact that Trace had likely spent several days there—given the realm's unique time flow—would only intensify her anguish.

"Guys!" Kire called out.

Startled, they turned to him, realizing he was several feet away, carefully moving around the sinkhole's perimeter, peering down into it. "Am I crazy, or...?"

"Whatever you're about to say, don't shout it out for everyone to hear!" Kaos interrupted, taking Amberly's hand and pulling her with him to join Kire so they could converse privately.

"I wasn't going to," Kire retorted, clearly annoyed.

"What is it? Did you find something?" Amberly asked.

"Do you guys feel that?" Kire asked, his voice tinged with concern.

After Amberly snatched her hand away from Kaos—he hadn't realized he had still been holding it—he stood very still, trying to feel whatever it was Kire was feeling. He carefully studied the expression on Kire's face, trying to figure it out. Kire looked astonished, as if he was experiencing something surreal. Kaos didn't exactly know what to make of it, but then, suddenly, he felt it, too. It was particularly difficult to describe—the sensation flowing through his body, as if he could physically feel some sort of magical energy radiating straight from the earth, from the hole. But it didn't make much sense; the earth itself wasn't supposed to be made of magic or contain magic inside the crust. But still, Kaos moved closer to the edge.

"What are you doing?!" Amberly whispered urgently. Along with her, others called out to him, telling him to stop. Kaos ignored all of them. He approached the edge, the tips of his black boots dangling off the edge. One little slip, one little crumble of the pavement, and he would go down inside it.

"It's stronger the closer you get to it," he said, trying to speak quietly to avoid anyone growing suspicious of what they were up to.

"Great. Now get back here," Amberly's face had a hint of worry.

For a moment, Kaos studied her, noticing how obvious it was that she was concerned about him. He couldn't be entirely alone in thinking that there was something between the two of them, not when she looked at him like that.

Not wanting to upset her further, he stepped back, and Amberly visibly relaxed. On the other side of the tape, people continued telling them to get out of there.

"What do you think that means?" Kire asked in a low voice.

"I don't know," Kaos admitted. But it felt to him as if maybe, possibly, deep down inside that sinkhole, something sinister yet magical and powerful awaited. He couldn't help but feel as though if he were to slide down to the bottom of it, he'd be pulled in, and on the other side would be something huge.

Kire looked over his shoulder, then over the other one, scanning the crowd as if trying to find a familiar face.

"I don't think she's here, Kire." Kaos wanted Kire to focus on the matter at hand, not look for Rose. He wanted to know where she ran off to as well, but they were a little busy trying to figure out how to save the universe.

"I'm sorry," Kire said, wincing slightly. As if ashamed. "But I've got to get out of here."

"*What*?" Amberly snapped. "Why? Where do you need to go? Don't leave us."

"I've got to talk to Rose's parents. I've got to do *something*. I can't focus on anything until I figure out where she is. I don't have a good feeling about it. I can't be the only one." Kire stared at the two of them, searching their expressions to see if they were just as worried.

Kaos looked at Amberly, who was staring at her feet.

Kire stood taller, resolved. "We'll talk more about this later."

"Kire, come on!" Kaos yelled, but Kire had already started jogging away from them, leaving Kaos and Amberly alone.

Kaos slowly turned back to Amberly, who looked like a lost puppy.

"All right then," he said, shoving his hands in his pockets. "I guess... it's just us right now."

"What do we do now, then?" Amberly replied, still not making eye contact with him.

Kaos looked back over at the sinkhole.

"Don't even *think* about going near it again," she barked.

"Why not?" Kaos asked. His curiosity was getting the better of him. He wanted to draw some sort of truth from her—or anything at all. But it was like trying to pull the sword from the stone.

"Maybe because you could fall to your death, and then we'd have one less Defender, making defeating Yash impossible."

Kaos rolled his eyes. "You don't have to worry about me."

"Yes, I do."

Finally, she met his eyes. Hers were stormy and fierce, just like she was. The wind picked up around them, whipping her hair back, her facial features fully exposed. She was so beautiful to Kaos that it hurt to look at her.

"Aren't you too busy worrying about Trace?" The bitterness was clear in his tone.

Amberly's shoulders slumped. "Can we... Can we go somewhere and talk? I think it's about time we hash everything out."

Finally.

Without saying a word, he nodded, and it was Amberly who led the way. They left the crowd, left the scene of the sinkhole and the chaos surrounding it.

They walked for a while in silence, and Kaos wondered where exactly Amberly was leading him. They had passed so many potential private spots to converse: an alleyway, a bench, a quiet coffee shop.

What she chose instead was a children's playground with a pair of swings. They were set further apart, in a separate sandbox away from the jungle gym. A few kids played around on it while their parents talked worriedly on their phones to their loved ones about the sinkhole. They were all far enough away not to be a nuisance while Amberly and Kaos had their talk.

"Swings?" Kaos asked, arching an eyebrow. He hadn't sat on one of those in years.

"What's wrong with swings?" Amberly asked, grabbing onto the rusty chains and taking a seat. Sighing, Kaos repeated the motion, and they sort of just pushed off the sand with their feet and swayed, getting close to bumping into each other. Kaos was waiting for Amberly to speak first, but when some time passed, he wondered if maybe *she* was waiting for *him* to speak first.

"So," he began at the same time Amberly finally lifted her head and said, "Kaos, listen—"

They both stopped speaking at the same time, too, then they broke into nervous laughter. But while Kaos's laughter quickly died away, Amberly's turned into tears.

"What is it?" Kaos asked, not liking the feeling inside his stomach, as though he had a bug, like he was going to throw up. And his chest... He felt a squeezing sensation as if something was gripping his heart tightly. He didn't like it one bit.

"Oh, Kaos. Why did you do it?"

Amberly hung her head and continued to sway. Kaos, on the other hand, had gone very still.

"What do you mean?" he asked.

"With me and Trace. I mean, I know *why* you did it. That was a dumb way to phrase the question. I just... I guess I just want to know why you were even willing to risk ruining everything. Ruining us. *All* of us."

"To be honest with you, Amberly, I wasn't thinking much at all. I was just... reacting."

It felt strange to finally be able to admit the truth, to finally come out with it. He knew what this talk was about; he knew this was his last chance to try and get what he wanted. It was now or never, so he couldn't lie anymore. He couldn't manipulate his way into Amberly's heart. If he was truly going to win her over, it would have to be with whatever he said right now.

"You made me feel like an idiot," Amberly told him.

Ouch. That was not what I had been hoping for.

He tried to redeem himself. "But I just thought that if..."

"If what?" she asked. "If you pushed us apart, I'd be more than open and willing to start dating you instead of Trace? That I'd be over him in an instant and ready to date his best friend? Trace and I were together for a long time. I know you don't know what it's like to be in love, but to teach you a little something about it, feelings don't just disappear because two people break up. It hurts. He hurt me. You hurt me. And I'm already dealing with so much on top of it all."

"I was just raised to go after what I want, okay?" He didn't want to apologize for that. It was one of the life lessons he appreciated his parents instilling in him. "Sometimes you *gotta* fight for it. Sometimes, you gotta take that risk. Sometimes, you gotta act now and think about the consequences later. And that's what I did."

"Are you not at all sorry?"

"Are *you* not at all interested in being with me?" he replied.

"I'm sorry, Kaos, but no," Amberly replied, staring him dead in the face as she said the words.

In a world full of so much uncertainty, how sure Amberly was of this statement couldn't be clearer to Kaos.

He and Amberly would never work. Amberly only wanted Trace, and maybe she would only *ever* want Trace. Maybe they'd be one of those few couples who made it through high school and college and married each other—high school sweethearts. And maybe Kaos would just become a memory, a friend the two of them once had a long, long time ago—the friend who tried to come between what was unbreakable.

"Then fine," Kaos said, clearing his throat and getting to his feet. The wind picked up further, sending a chill down his spine and causing him to shudder. "I am... sorry. I guess I'll just stop trying."

"I think you need to," she agreed. "Things are better the way they were before. I just want to get back to that."

Kaos understood, but it didn't make it hurt any less. Going back to the past was exactly where he *didn't* want to be. But what choice did he have?

10

ater that night, Kaos lay on his bed in complete darkness, with the only light coming from the glowing screen on his phone as he sent messages back and forth in the group chat. The only person responding to him was Amberly. Half the day had passed since their earlier conversation, but Kaos was still reeling from it. He didn't feel like doing anything, not even his homework, practicing with his crown, or figuring out what to do about the massive sinkhole. But Amberly was being herself, demanding a response from someone. When he finally started replying, she had just sent the text.

Amberly: Am I just sitting here talking to myself?

Kaos: We're going to figure out a plan. It's allllll good, Amber. Chilllll.

Amberly: Chill?! Good joke. Sooooo funny. Kire isn't the only one who felt something at the sinkhole. If only he'd REPLY to this group text so I could confirm that I felt the same thing as him!

Amberly: Kire! Text us back.

> Kaos: You better listen to her, dude. She's gonna
> show up at your house.

Not even ten seconds passed before Amberly texted again.

Amberly: I cannot believe you're ignoring us, Kire.
This could be the start of the END of the WORLD.
Did YOU feel something, Kaos? It was like a weird
buzzing feeling in my bones. IDK. I don't know
how to describe it.

> Kaos: You're not alone. I felt it, too. So I'm
> guessing that's what Kire felt.

Amberly: It was Yash. That's the only explanation.
Right? Everyone else I've talked to hasn't
mentioned anything about feeling weird energy
around the sinkhole. And this chick from the cheer
squad was literally standing right behind the
caution tape. I saw it on her social media.

> Kaos: I feel like you want me to say that it's still a
> possibility that it wasn't Yash. But to be honest
> with you, I'm pretty sure you're right. It was Yash.

Amberly: !!!

Amberly: So this is it, then? The world is literally
ending. It's started. What are we going to do?
Kire, what is Halo's status? I'm freaking out here!

Kaos' stomach dipped. He preferred to think Amberly was just being dramatic about the whole thing, but in reality, she was acting typically, the appropriate way for somebody to react to such an awful situation. Everybody else in the world thought the sinkhole was just an unfortunate natural phenomenon. To them, it sucked that it happened, and it sucked for those who got hurt and lost their property and belongings down inside of it. But *they* were thinking ahead about the future, about how they would get past it. Little did they know that unless these five teenagers could save them, there was no future.

The nausea was back and stronger than ever, and Kaos had to sit up, debating whether he should run to his bathroom or wait it out. He felt clammy, and his head was pounding.

> Amberly: Kaos.

> Amberly: Don't tell me you've fallen asleep. How can you sleep when the world is literally on the brink of devastation?

Kaos checked the time of his last response. It had only been two minutes. He sighed and replied.

> Kaos: I'm not sleeping. But maybe since it's just the two of us talking, we should get off the group chat.

Seconds later, he had a text from a different thread, but it was still from Amberly. Their conversation was now private.

> Amberly: Obviously Trace isn't gonna text us. He doesn't have service in the other realm.

> Kaos: I know.

> Amberly: He doesn't know about the sinkhole. He doesn't know what's happening.

> Kaos: You're just searching for a reason to go and see him.

But the more Kaos thought about it, the more Amberly was

right. He was just bitter about being rejected by Amberly. They did need to go find Trace and tell him what happened. He was going to have to come back and fight, whether he liked it or not. Kaos would drag him out of the Albus realm if he had to. Without their group complete, they were doomed.

Hopefully, Kire figured out where Rose went.

Amberly: Fine. Don't come. I'll go alone.

Kaos: I never said I wouldn't come with you. Tomorrow. OK?

Amberly: Now.

Kaos: We might need the extra help convincing him to come back. Tomorrow. Since Kire is ignoring our texts, we have to find him in person and bring him with us. Good night.

Kaos's phone continued to buzz, but instead of reading any more of Amberly's anxious responses, he simply shoved his phone under the pillow on the far side of his king-sized bed and let the darkness take him over.

When he woke up the next day, his phone had all sorts of notifications, not just from Amberly. There were news updates, group texts with other kids at school, and social media posts. As Kaos yawned and skimmed the notifications, he could make out that it was no longer the sinkhole everyone was freaking out about. The topic of worry had seemingly moved on to Charlie Rose.

Kaos clicked on an article link.

Amid a series of unsettling events plaguing the otherwise tranquil town of Montgomery, a junior at Saint Bernard High School has been reported missing following a bizarre incident involving a massive sinkhole that abruptly opened up on a bustling city street. The disappearance of the young girl has added yet another layer of concern to a community already grappling with its fair share of misfortune. Montgomery, a town known for its serenity, has recently faced a string of unusual incidents that have left its residents on edge. Just a short while ago, a relentless forest fire raged through The White Forest, requiring heroic efforts from local firefighters and first responders to finally bring it under control. Authorities were baffled by the fire's ferocity and mysterious origin. Adding to the town's woes, Saint Bernard High School has been hit with a rash of break-ins, leaving school officials and parents deeply troubled by security breaches. The string of deaths remains under investigation, with no leads to date. Now, as the community reels from these unsettling events, a sense of unease deepens with the disappearance of Charlie Rose from Saint Bernard High School. Her sudden vanishing act has raised questions about the connection between these seemingly unrelated incidents, leaving Montgomery residents seeking answers and authorities working tirelessly to uncover the truth.

Some of the speculation on social media filled Kaos's stomach with more unease. The majority of his peers seemed to think that Rose must've been standing right there when the sinkhole happened and that she was likely long gone, buried deep into the earth. Things were worse than Kaos anticipated. He thought he'd wake up this morning and find that there was a simple explanation as to why they hadn't found Rose yesterday or why Kire hadn't responded to any of their messages from last night. But Rose was still missing.

She can't be dead, Kaos thought to himself as he got ready for school in a hurry since he didn't hear his alarm with the phone shoved under his pillow. *We'd know if she died. We're connected by our gifts.* He wasn't sure *how* he'd know, but he was certain that there would be some telling sign. Rose had to still be alive. But where was she?

Kaos didn't even bother trying to text Kire again this time—he wasn't normally one to make phone calls, but he figured this matter warranted one.

And he definitely wasn't the kind to ever leave a voicemail, but when Kire annoyingly didn't answer, Kaos felt as though it was his only option.

"Dude. *What* is going on? The news says Rose is missing. Everyone's freaking out. Why are you being so impossible to get a hold of? Answer your freaking phone."

Growling, he threw his phone into his backpack aggressively and rushed off to pick up Amberly and then go to school. He didn't bother trying to pick up Kire at his house because he was sure they wouldn't get a response from him there either. Kire probably wasn't even home. He was probably out in The White Forest, looking for the *love of his life.*

"He better be here," Amberly said through her teeth as Kaos pulled into the student parking lot. She unbuckled her seatbelt and was out of the car in the blink of an eye, and Kaos nearly had a jog to keep up with her as she stormed to the front of the school, her eyes scanning the crowd of students. Kaos noticed instantly how sad everyone looked. He saw faces with tears. He heard whispers of woe. He only wanted to roll his eyes because he felt it was all an act. No one *actually* cared about Rose. She hardly had any friends. All these kids wanted was to be consoled by the disappearance of somebody else. All these kids wanted was to turn it into being about *them.*

I'm sick of high school, he thought.

"There he is!" Amberly screeched, gripping Kaos's arm and digging her fingernails into his skin as she pulled him along to the side of the greenhouse. How Amberly was able to spot Kire from so far away was unknown to Kaos, but he was grateful for Amberly. And he was annoyed at Kire for ignoring them for such a long time.

"What the heck, dude," Kaos said when they reached him. Kire was slumped on the bench outside of the greenhouse, where he and Rose were often seen sitting and talking.

"They don't even know," Kire mumbled, hanging his head and refusing to look at them. He was wearing the same clothes he had on the day before. His hair was disheveled. He had blotches of dirt on his knees and elbows and under his jaw.

"Kire?" Amberly asked, sounding more concerned than angry. "Were you... out all night?"

"I can't do it," Kire continued to mutter, shaking his head. He was talking so quietly that Kaos could barely hear him. He stayed back, sensing that Kire didn't want to be messed with, letting Amberly take the lead with this.

"Can't do what?" Amberly asked timidly, taking a cautious step closer to him.

"I can't go in there."

"What do you mean?"

He snapped his head up so abruptly that it almost made Kaos flinch. "I can't go in there!" He pointed at the school with a shaking finger. "Rose is *missing*, and I'm the only one who *actually* cares! They're all faking it! Even her parents! Her parents don't even care!"

Amberly and Kaos exchanged looks. Before they could even explain to Kire their plan to go and see Trace, he got up and stormed off toward the soccer field.

He wasn't in a much better mood when lunch rolled around. Thankfully, he hadn't ditched school entirely, but it was clear as day that he did not want to be there. He kept his head down at the lunch table. Kaos gathered he probably didn't want to look up and see someone fake crying over their lost "friend."

Just because it would be amusing to Kaos, he thought about using his crown to manipulate someone into causing a scene, just to see how Kire would react. But this wasn't the time for jokes and games. Besides, he wouldn't have anyone to laugh with. Trace was in the Albus realm, completely clueless about everything happening here.

When Amberly showed up at the table with a tray full of food she never normally ate, Kaos stared at her in surprise.

She set the tray down in front of Kire and pushed it in his direction. Her movements were slow and cautious, as if he were going to reach out and bite her at any moment. He was a coiled snake, full of venom.

"You should eat something," she said in a soft voice. She sounded nurturing, which was so unlike Amberly that Kaos had to do a double take to make sure he really was standing beside her. He hadn't sat down at the table yet because he wasn't sure if Kire *wanted* to be joined. But he followed Amberly's lead when she sat down across from Kire, and he took a seat next to her.

On top of the table in the bustling, louder-than-usual cafeteria, Kire had a paused video pulled up on his phone screen. "I don't want to eat," he said darkly.

"I get that," Amberly said. "But you still need to. You need your strength, Kire. And you need sleep. And... And I spent my own money getting you all this food because I have no idea what you like, so you better not let it go to waste!"

Knowing better than to disobey Amberly, Kire gingerly reached out for a french fry and popped it in his mouth, chewing it slowly as if he were eating cardboard instead.

"What's that on your phone?" Kaos asked, nodding his head toward the glowing device.

Kire pushed the phone in Kaos's direction. "Just watch it."

Kaos read the headline of the news article above the paused video. *Desperate Plea: Missing Girl's Parents Release Emotional Video Seeking Answers.*

This ought to be good, he thought.

Surrounded by microphones and flashing cameras, standing on the front porch of their home, a man and a woman blinked rapidly and shared anxious glances at each other. It was the woman, very short and very strict-looking, who cleared her throat and leaned into the microphone first.

"Um, hi. My name is Beverly Rose," Rose's mother said, her voice quivering as she reached for her husband's hand and held it tightly for everyone to see. Her eyes went to the camera, big and fearful. "And this is my husband, Tim Rose." She paused to take a deep breath, and it looked to Kaos as though she was struggling to keep her composure. "Our daughter, Charlie, is everything to us. She's a bright, beautiful young girl with dreams and aspirations."

Tim nodded, the also-short man adjusting his tie and getting ready to speak next. When he did, his voice choked with emotion. "Charlie, or Rose, since I know you prefer to be called that, if you're out there, please know how much we love you. We miss you so much, sweetheart." His voice cracked, and then he swallowed hard. His eyes lined with tears. "We'd give anything to have you back. Anything at all. Please, if anyone knows anything, come forward. Our family is incomplete without her."

Kaos watched Beverly's grip on Tim's hand tighten as she wiped her own tears. "Charlie—*Rose*—we're not angry. We just... We want to know that you're safe. That you're okay. We'll do whatever it takes to bring you home." She turned her gaze back to the camera, her eyes pleading. "Please, help us find our daughter."

Kaos swallowed the lump that formed in his throat. He had expected to see something entirely different. As far as he knew, Rose wasn't close with her family. But right there, on that screen, showed two humans who were living a parent's nightmare. It seemed real to Kaos. Raw.

But when he stole a glance at Kire, he had the feeling he was wrong or that Kire thought differently. His eyebrows were furrowed deeply, his eyes dark.

"Huh," Kaos said, having to clear his throat to get rid of the emotion he felt welling up inside him because of the video. "I don't know." He slid the phone back over to Kire. "It seemed pretty genuine to me."

Amberly nodded slowly beside him, having watched the video over his shoulder.

Kire was silent for a moment. "It's because they know how to put on a show," he said in that same low, dark voice from earlier by the greenhouse. Kaos had never seen Kire like this. He hardly even recognized him.

"You don't think..." Amberly started.

Kire knew what she wanted to say. He cut her off with a sharp shake of his head. "I *know* it's all a bunch of lies. It's all for show."

"I don't know, they seem *really* devastated." Amberly cringed as she said it, as if she was expecting a blow afterward.

"Come on! Look at them!" Kire shouted loudly. "Yeah, they *seem* devastated. But they're lying!"

"Hey, dude, come on," Kaos said, stepping in. "We believe you, okay?"

Kire shook his head repeatedly, getting up from the table. "I've got to get her back."

"Where are you going?" Amberly asked, getting to her feet as well. Kire didn't answer her. He stormed away yet again, Amberly going after him for only a few steps before she decided to give up and let him go.

She groaned loudly in frustration and spun around to Kaos, dejectedly slapping her hands to her sides. "Great. Until we fix *that* issue, there's no way we can leave to talk to Trace."

For the first time in a while, Amberly and Kaos were finally on the same page about something.

11

Kaos wasn't typically the type of person to feel stress, but he was certainly starting to feel it now. As the day continued, Kire was nowhere to be located, yet Amberly was insistent on finding him and equally insistent on making sure Kaos helped her with it. It was a lot for Kaos to deal with. He had a pounding headache because he had been reduced to using his crown to manipulate anyone he saw causing a fuss about Rose's disappearance, *just* in case Kire happened upon them and accused them of faking it. Kaos expected that the small outburst at lunch was only a fragment of the huge meltdown Kire was moments away from having, and Kaos felt it was his job to ensure that he stopped it any way he could. He couldn't believe he was actually using his powers to *help* Kire. He couldn't believe he was using them for something other than defeating Yash or for his own personal gain. But anything to give him a little less to deal with right now was actually beneficial for Kaos—every single person in The Unlikely Defenders was giving him grief. Amberly with her heightened stress and the need to be more dramatic about everything than necessary—not to mention being rejected by her was still very fresh, and Kaos didn't feel quite right about it, but he also didn't have any time to process it, either.

Then there was Kire; it was like he was a completely different person, like they had lost their club's vice president. Like Heno took him over just as he took over Andrew and turned him into a raging, hungry monster. With Kire so worried about Rose, so desperate to find her, and so mad at everyone else for pretending to care about her, he probably wasn't paying any attention to Halo. The old relic was likely inside Kire's book bag at that very moment, being completely ignored. And it stressed Kaos out because what if Halo had given them a warning about Yash's arrival? He thought it likely that Kire hadn't even *glanced* at the thing over the past twenty-four hours. Each time Kaos thought about the unopened book, his stomach dipped.

Then, with Trace—Kaos was stressed because he knew all of this would be easier if Trace was there with him, helping Kaos get ahold of Amberly and Kire, helping Kaos in getting them to keep it together. Kaos needed that camaraderie again. He needed his friend back. But he had a feeling getting him to come back to Montgomery wasn't going to be an easy task.

Then there was Rose. Why was she missing? Why *now*? And what on Earth had happened? Did it have to do with Yash or not? Was she okay? Were they going to have to take on Yash without her? Would it even be possible?

On top of that, Kaos was the leader of The Unlikely Defenders. He was supposed to be strategizing, getting the others to all train with their gifts, and figuring out exactly how they were going to go about a battle against the entity that was Yash. But he had absolutely no time to plan, no time to prep, no time to even *think* about what they'd do if more sinkholes started popping up and the world began to crumble. He couldn't even comprehend what kind of powers someone like Yash might have, but he could guess that all of the minions they had defeated didn't hold a candle to what Yash would bring to the table.

And possibly the worst part of it all was that none of this would've happened if Rezin hadn't read Kaos's mind and impaled himself on Trace's sword in the first place. Kaos should've never tried to infiltrate; he should have shut off his ability the moment he felt the pain and realized that something wasn't right during their battle. But since Kaos was so stubborn, so intent on fighting for what he wanted, he ignored the warnings, and because of it, everything crumbled.

When school ended, Kaos and Amberly decided that Kire must have left campus entirely at lunch—he had not been in any other classes, and he had not been in the hallways or even in any of the bathrooms; Kaos had checked them all.

He and Amberly stood in front of the school as everyone left for the day, and Kaos rubbed his tender temples with his pointer fingers while Amberly tapped her foot and stared around at the throng of students.

"I don't like what you told me about Halo," she said to Kaos after a moment. Kaos had filled her in on his worry about whether or not Kire was remembering to keep an eye out for Halo's warning. "I hadn't even been thinking about Halo, to be honest. But you're probably right. Kire has probably forgotten all about that stupid book. Kaos, we *need* to find him."

"Tell me something I don't know," Kaos said.

"What's wrong with you?" she snapped, as if angry at him for having a headache.

"Nothing. I'm fine." He stopped rubbing his temples and rolled his shoulders back. "He's gotta be around here somewhere. Let's check the most obvious possibility."

"His *house*?"

It looked like the last thing Amberly wanted to do. She bit down on her thumbnail, apprehensive about it. Rolling his eyes, Kaos grabbed her elbow, dragging her over to his dad's car.

"Come on, let's just get it over with."

When they knocked on the Hunters' front door, Amberly

crossed her fingers and squeezed her eyes shut, bouncing on the balls of her feet.

"Please be here, please be here, *please* be hereeee."

Did Amberly want to find Kire so that they could sooner get to the Albus realm? Back to Trace?

When the door cracked open, it was Kire's mom who answered.

"Mrs. Hunter?" Amberly asked, sounding shy. Mrs. Hunter was a small woman with dark skin, dark eyes, dark hair, and thin lips. She didn't smile when she saw them.

"You're Kire's friend, right?" she asked, her eyes zeroing in on Amberly. "And you're..."

"I'm Amberly, yes."

Kaos stood there, feeling awkward about the interaction. He hadn't really thought about what a significant moment it would be if Amberly and Emma came face-to-face.

Some silence passed between them all as Amberly and Kire's mom stared at each other, and Kaos tried to look at *anything* else, as if that would give them some privacy.

"Is Kire here?" he eventually said to break the tension.

"I'm afraid he's not," Emma said, still not opening the door any wider.

"Have you talked to him?" Kaos asked.

"A little bit. But... he's been awfully busy looking for Rose. He's worried sick."

"Oh, *we* know," Amberly said, her eyes bugging out of her head.

Emma went back to staring at her. "The two of you have been hanging out, correct?"

Amberly nodded.

Emma clicked her tongue and eyed Amberly up and down again as if she couldn't believe what she was seeing. "Gerald's not here either," she said. "Just me in this house. I—just so you know, Amberly, I cannot forgive him for what he's done. For making you live the life you have when he had the power to make sure you were much more comfortable."

Amberly's mouth opened and closed for a while.

"It's not your fault, Mrs. Hunter," she eventually said. "And I really appreciate you sticking up for me."

"I'm just ashamed it took me so long to get rid of him."

The two shared a slight smile.

But this wasn't the time for that.

"Do you know where we might find Kire?" Kaos asked, wanting to move the conversation along.

"I'm not sure," Emma replied. "Maybe try all the places he and Rose have gone together? I'm sure that boy would go to the end of the earth to look for her."

It was *not* what Kaos wanted to hear.

"Well, thanks anyway," Amberly said, still sounding weirdly shy.

Emma beamed at her for a moment, then nodded at Kaos. "I'll tell him that you're looking for him if he comes home."

"Thanks," Kaos said.

When Emma closed the door, he and Amberly turned away and walked down the front path. Amberly chewed on her bottom lip, lost in thought.

"What is it?" Kaos asked. Why did her eyes look... misty? Why was her lower lip trembling?

"I just... I don't know," Amberly croaked. "That was weird."

"Because of your dad?"

She nodded, unable to speak. A single tear slid down her cheek, but then she held her breath for a long time, and Kaos just stood beside her, not having the slightest clue what to do next.

"Let's go to Trace's," Amberly suddenly said, looking much more collected than she had just seconds ago.

"Wait, what?" Kaos asked.

"We'll walk over there, and hopefully, on the way, we'll find Kire. But we need to check on Trace's mom. She's probably worried about Trace since he hasn't been home, and there's a missing girl. One who Trace has been hanging out with."

She had a point.

"All right," Kaos agreed. "But we'll look for him from inside the car. I'm not walking."

As they drove through Montgomery toward Trace's house, they both kept their eyes peeled for any signs of Kire. Kaos also kept an eye out for Rose, too, just in case.

They made it all the way to Trace's house without signs of either of them.

"Do you think maybe... Trace might be inside?" Amberly asked, not moving to get out of the front seat once Kaos parked the car. "Do you think there's a chance he came back?"

"Is that why you wanted to come here?"

"No. My first thought really was that we needed to check on his mom. But that thought did come after."

"He has to know he can't stay in that realm forever," Kaos told her, trying to be reassuring. Amberly said nothing, so Kaos unbuckled his seatbelt and got out of the car. Before he shut the door, he waited for her to do the same.

"You coming?" he asked.

Wordlessly, she finally buckled her seatbelt and got out as well, and the two approached the house together. Before they could reach the steps, the door opened, and Vivian stepped out wearing a nightgown, barefooted.

"Hi, Mrs. Henderson," Amberly said.

"Hey, Viv," Kaos said.

"Hello again," Vivian replied.

Kaos sighed, trying to determine which side of Vivian he was going to get today. Was she drunk, or was she sober?

"H-how are you doing?" Amberly asked.

"Well, I haven't touched another drink since you all last left here, if that's what you're *really* wondering," she replied. "Trace isn't with you, is he? He hasn't been home since then."

Amberly and Kaos looked at each other. Then Kaos turned back to Trace's mom. "He's back at my house," he replied quickly, coming up with an excuse. "He's been staying with me. He... sent us to check on you, to make sure you're okay and that you've been taking your medicine."

"Really?" she asked, squinting at him. "He's been with you? Why hasn't he gone to school?"

"I..."

She continued. "School's been calling me, telling me he's been absent."

Kaos had to lay it on thick. "Well... what did you expect?" She needed the hard truth. "He's pretty upset at you. He doesn't even want to go to school. He's too depressed."

"I had a slipup. *One* slipup. Tell him that I haven't had another. Will you? Tell him I'm fine. *Ugh*, I'm just *so* glad to hear that he's okay. I know that your other friend is missing, and I was worried that—*no*. He's fine. Everything is *fine*."

"So... you haven't heard from Trace, like, at all?" Amberly asked, causing Vivian to grow a confused expression. "I... just told him to text you to check in, and he said he would, so maybe he was lying to me," she finished with a lie.

"I haven't heard a word," Vivian said. "He hasn't even come back to grab anything. I don't think he's—I'm *guessing* he hasn't gone to work either. He probably doesn't even have his job anymore."

"Hey, this might be a long shot," Kaos tried, swiftly changing the subject, "but our other friend, Kire, hasn't stopped by here, has he?"

Vivian pursed her lips and shook her head. "He hasn't. Why, has *he* gone missing, too?"

"No, nothing like that," Amberly said quickly.

"Are you sure?" Vivian stared more closely at them. "Are you two... all right?"

Far from it, Kaos thought.

"We are," he said aloud. "I'll tell Trace what you said. I'm sure he'll come home soon."

Vivian still looked skeptical, but she let it slide, and Amberly and Kaos said their goodbyes and left.

When they got back inside Kaos's dad's car, their phones, which were sitting in the cupholders between them, beeped and buzzed repeatedly, lighting up with notification after notification, just as Kaos's phone had done earlier that morning.

They picked up their phones and looked at the screens. Apparently, there was a video about Kire spreading to all of their classmates like wildfire. It was all anyone wanted to talk about.

"I don't even know if I wanna watch it," Amberly said. Kaos ignored her and opened one of the many messages he received from multiple people containing the video.

It wasn't clear when the video was taken, but it was easy to tell that the footage was shot outside of Rose's home. Many people still lingered outside even though a press conference was no longer being held. Whoever was recording quickly shifted the camera, and Kire came into view, his fists balled and his face red as he stormed up the street, ignoring everyone trying to ask him questions and get comments about the disappearance of his girlfriend. He stormed right up to the front door and pounded on it. To Kire, it didn't matter that Rose's parents had asked for privacy during this difficult time.

Tim Rose opened the door first, Beverly Rose standing close behind him.

"Tell everyone the truth!" Kire bellowed, getting as close to their faces as he could without stepping inside their house. "Go on!"

In the video, they were too far away for Kaos to make out what Rose's parents said back to him; *they* were talking in normal voices. Kire's yelling was the only thing that could be clearly heard.

"You never cared about her!" Kire went on. "You've made her life miserable for years! Do you know how many tears she's cried over you for how you treat her?! Of course not! Why would you?! You better get out here and come clean. Tell everyone about how you prefer your other daughter over her. How I had to spend *hours* convincing you to even file the report in the first place!"

In the doorway, Beverly broke down into tears. Not even Tim

looked angry as he stared at his daughter's boyfriend, letting him scream in his face.

As Kire kept screaming at them, people finally decided to do something about it, and a handful of strangers pulled Kire back away from the house. Kire struggled against them and tried to get free, and even after Rose's parents closed the door, Kire kept yelling.

Then, the video ended.

Kaos thought that their effort seemed futile now to figure out where Kire was. His mother didn't know where to find him, so how were *they* supposed to figure it out?

"I don't know where I'm supposed to look." Kaos sighed in frustration, gripping the steering wheel of his dad's car tightly as he and Amberly continued driving around, searching for Kire. "How are we supposed to have any idea of the kind of places Kire and Rose went together?" He clenched his teeth as he spoke. "If he would just stop being like this."

"Kaos"—Amberly lightly touched Kaos's arm—"remember what you texted me yesterday about needing to chill?"

He shot her a look.

She nodded. "You need to take your own advice right about now." She didn't sound snooty in her tone; she was being genuine, offering advice in the best way she could: by being direct.

"I know. But—there's just so many other things we could be doing. You said so yourself last night—the world could be *literally* about to fall apart. If Yash can create a sinkhole like that, what else can he do? Can he cause hurricanes? Tornadoes? Wildfires bigger than the one Trace started?"

Amberly swallowed and sat back in her seat. "I know. I get it. It's scary. But freaking out isn't going to do either of us any good. And you're the one who said it was better if we found Kire first before going to talk to Trace."

"I know." He sighed again as they rolled up to a stoplight. Amberly turned and looked out the window again for any signs of Kire. Kaos was too busy thinking about how pathetic it would be if they ended up having to take on Yash with just the two of them. If they didn't reunite with the other Unlikely Defenders soon, they had no chance. No hope.

"Can't you just... I don't know, use your powers to try to read the mind of somebody who might've seen Kire recently?" Amberly asked. "Or Rose, even? There's got to be somebody who knows where they went."

"It doesn't work like that. I can't just reach out into the unknown and try to find a random person's thoughts."

She crossed her arms and huffed. "Well, that's... stupid."

"What about *you* then, huh? Can't *you* just put on your gauntlet and use telekinesis to lift the earth where Kire is standing—since you can't use your powers on him directly—and fly him back over to us?"

"Okay, that would be even *stupider*."

The light turned green, and Kaos resumed driving, trying a different route than the one they had been circling. It was starting to get late. He needed to get home soon, at least so he could manipulate his parents into not realizing that he had even left in the first place.

"Kaos, stop!" Amberly shrieked.

Startled, Kaos swerved left and right, nearly losing control of the car for a moment before finally pumping the brakes. They came to a stop on the side of the road.

"What the heck, Amberly?!" he shouted. "You can't just yell like that when I'm in the middle of driving!"

She ignored him, unbuckling her seatbelt and flinging the car door open, her movements urgent.

"Amberly!" he yelled after her. She had left the door wide open and was sprinting into the trees. They were at the edge of The White Forest, a part of it Kaos wasn't too familiar with.

Not even bothering to turn the car off, he parked it and jumped out to run after her.

"Amberly, where are you going?!"

"I saw him!" she yelled over her shoulder. "I saw him right before he darted into the forest!"

"Kire!" Kaos shouted. "We need to talk to you! It's urgent!"

He caught up to Amberly with ease and kept pace with her as they weaved around trees and their roots.

"Are you sure it was him?" he asked her.

"Kire!" she continued to call, not answering his question.

When a figure stepped out from behind a large tree trunk, Amberly and Kaos nearly slammed into them. Instead, the pair screeched to a halt, slightly out of breath. In front of them, Kire's chest was heaving rapidly as well.

"Why are you following me?!" he barked at them. "Didn't you get the hint? Leave me alone. I don't wanna talk to anyone until I find her."

"Kire, you're being *seriously* idiotic," Amberly snapped, crossing her arms. "We're sort of a package deal here, *hello*? Did you forget what's coming? Have you even checked on Halo lately? God, Kire, I know you're worried about Rose, but there are other things you need to deal with, too!"

"Of course I've checked Halo," Kire bit out. "I check the dang book every two minutes, trying to stop myself from doing something I'll regret."

"What are you talking about?" Amberly asked.

Kaos, quick to understand, answered for Kire. "He's been thinking about asking Halo to find her."

Amberly gasped.

Staring back at them, Kire couldn't hide the shadow of guilt that crept across his face.

"You can't do that!" Amberly shrieked. "Kire, Halo can't be touched until it's time for the big warning about Yash. Here—give me the book so you can't be tempted." She held out her hand.

"Not a chance," he said, staggering backward. "I said I've been *thinking* about it. I haven't actually done it."

"And how are we supposed to stop you if you become too tempted again, when you keep running away from us and ignoring our texts and calls?"

"I'm starting to feel like there aren't any other options," Kire cried out. He looked lost, broken, torn apart. "I'm worried sick about her. I'm—I'm desperate to know if she's okay. And Halo... has the potential to give me the answers I'm looking for. I mean... Rose is the most important person in my life. I... I *love* her. But yet I have to remember that she doesn't matter as much as the collective universe matters. And I just—"

He cut himself off, hanging his head.

Kaos barely heard him when he muttered, "Maybe someone *should* take Halo away from me."

"I'm sorry, Kire," Amberly said, stepping toward him, "but I think it's for the best. At least for right now.

Still, Kire looked hesitant to hand Halo over to her.

"Guys," Kaos quipped loudly, an idea forming in his head. They both stared at him expectantly. "What if we find a different magical resource to help us locate Rose?"

"What kind of resource?" Amberly asked.

"I think we should go talk to Albus," Kaos revealed. "He might be able to help."

"D-do you really think that?" Kire asked, a flicker of hope passing through him.

"I think that it's worth trying," Kaos said with a shrug.

"Well, that works out perfectly then," Amberly said, clapping her hands together. "Because we need to go to the Albus realm anyway. We need to update Trace on everything."

Kire stared around.

"What?" Amberly asked.

"I feel weird about leaving. About not being able to keep getting updates about Rose once I'm inside the Albus realm."

"By the time we get back, we will have been gone in this world for, like, a few seconds," Amberly said. "It'll be fine, Kire." She walked around behind him, pulled his backpack off his shoulders, and put it instead over hers. Kire didn't put up a fight. He didn't utter another word about it. Seeing it had Kaos wondering just how close Kire had come to using Halo to find Rose, to jeopardizing their chances of saving the universe.

Because they had entered from this less familiar side of the forest, the journey to the cave was quicker than usual. And once they passed through the portal and were once again in the Albus realm, they found a blue stone perched on top of a flat boulder just beside the arch.

"Trace... left this here?" Amberly asked. She slowly picked it up and squinted at it as if trying to verify that it was indeed the teleportation stone.

"He probably didn't think he had a need for it anymore," Kaos said, "you know, with his decision to live here for the rest of his life."

"*Or* he just left it here because he knew we'd be needing it," Kire interjected, trying to prevent Amberly from having a meltdown over what Kaos said. Amberly had a watchful eye as she met Kaos's stare.

"It's not like I *want* him to stay here," Kaos clarified. "I want him home just as much as you do. I don't know if you've forgotten, but despite everything that's happened, he's still my best friend."

"Fine," Amberly replied, holding out the rock. "Just... don't be pessimistic. We *need* this to go well."

In agreement, Kaos touched the rock, and so did Kire. The sensation was quick, and Kaos was back on his feet in a millisecond. He felt as though his head had been jostled greatly, and his headache was worse than ever, so much so that he needed to sit down.

"Kaos?" Amberly asked, dropping to her knees in front of him when he fell on his butt into the dirt. They were in Novus's village, right on the outskirts, near the path to her cottage.

"My head," Kaos said, squeezing his eyes shut. He felt his crown pulled away from him, and when he opened his eyes, Amberly was holding it.

"I don't know," she said, holding it with only her pointer finger and her thumb as if she were holding a dead rat. "Maybe *this* is causing it."

Kaos had to admit that he did feel better already. Maybe the thing was squeezing his head too hard. Maybe it was too tight. Or maybe there was something wrong with its function ever since Rezin caused it to backfire.

"I'm gonna put it in Kire's bag, okay?" Amberly asked him.

Kaos nodded, allowing Kire to help him back to his feet.

"I haven't been feeling that great either," Kire said as they strolled along the path.

"Well, *yeah*, because you haven't eaten or slept since Rose disappeared," Kaos reminded him.

"What about you, Amberly?" Kire asked, ignoring Kaos's comment. "How have you been feeling? You know—physically?"

"Huh?"

Kire stopped walking and stared at her. "Did you really not just hear me? You were staring right at me."

Amberly shrugged. "Sorry. I was just... thinking. What did you ask?"

"Walk and talk," Kaos reminded them, moving ahead. It wasn't hard to guess what had Amberly so distracted. She was moments away from being reunited with Trace, whom, they all agreed, would likely be wherever Novus was. Perhaps Trace was even staying in her cottage with her. Her small, cozy, intimate cottage.

"Have you felt particularly drained lately?" Kire asked her again.

"Oh, yeah," she said. "But it's not too bad."

"I'm worried it has something to do with our gifts," Kire said. "First, it was just Rose getting those nosebleeds. But we've had so much drama going on lately... I don't know. It's just a thought."

"Oh, *great*," Kaos groaned. "So if we don't get along, not only do our powers suck, but our powers slowly begin to *kill* us, too?"

"I don't know," Kire said. "They really should have a rulebook for this."

"*How to Be an Unlikely Defender*," Kaos recited.

When the cottage came into view, Kaos and Kire started up the path to the front door. Amberly trailed behind. When the boys turned around and noticed her lagging, she simply crossed her arms and called to them, "You guys go. I'm just gonna stay right here."

"Suit yourself," Kire replied.

When they reached the door, Kaos pounded on it. "Trace. Are you in there?"

As luck would have it, Trace Henderson was the one to open it.

For a brief moment, Kaos almost didn't recognize him. He was dressed entirely in the type of clothing only worn in the Albus realm: a deep brown leather vest, a thin white long-sleeve shirt underneath it, and thick, polished boots.

"Oh, hey guys," Trace said with an air of casualness, as though he had invited them over for tea.

Behind him, Nova appeared, looking over his shoulder. "Oh, hello, everyone!" she said with a smile. "It's so good to see you all again."

Trace turned to her. "Is it all right if I let them in?"

"Certainly," she replied.

Once everyone was safely tucked away in the small space, including Amberly, Trace was the first to speak.

"So I'm guessing you have news to tell me. Has it started? Did Halo give Kire the warning?"

"Not yet," Kaos replied. "Something else has happened."

"Wait a moment," Novus interrupted, peering around at all of them. "Aren't you guys missing someone? Where is Rose?"

"That's... part of the problem," Kaos explained. "Trace, she's missing. And the whole town is freaking out about it."

"Yeah, and Kire is becoming famous for exploding on her parents and calling them out on how crappy they are." Amberly's arms were still crossed, and she still looked reserved and closed off, but she let out a brief snicker about the video.

"You guys know about that?" Kire asked, his cheeks turning pink.

"Wait, Rose is—she's missing, though?" Trace asked, his brows furrowing deeply. "What do you think could've happened? Where do you think she could be?"

"We don't know," Kire snapped.

Trace, who had made himself comfortable on the padded bench in Nova's seating area, sighed again. "When did it happen? How many days has it been in the Earth realm?"

"How many days has it been *here*?" Amberly asked back. "Your boots look pretty worn in. Your hair is getting long. And when's the last time you shaved?"

Trace stroked the stubble on his chin. "I lost track of time, honestly," he replied. "I didn't really think much about it because I knew that even though a lot of days were passing here, it couldn't have been too much time that passed on Earth, right?"

"It's been at least a week," Nova interjected. "Maybe a fortnight."

"What the heck is a *fortnight*?" Amberly asked. "Do you have that word written on your clock somewhere?"

"Clock?" Novus tilted her head and stared at Amberly.

"It's two weeks," Kire explained.

"Then just say that," Amberly muttered under her breath.

"Have you been staying here with Novus this whole time?" Kaos asked Trace, wanting to say something before Amberly's attitude notched up even higher.

"Guys," Kire snapped before Trace could answer. "We can catch up later. We've got to go find Albus, remember?"

"What for?" Trace asked.

"We're going to see if he can tell us where Rose is."

"I'm coming with then," Trace said automatically.

"Great. And does *Tinker Bell* here want to join as well?" Amberly asked.

"What on Earth is a 'Tinker Bell'? " Novus responded. Instead of replying, Amberly merely smirked at her while Trace shook his head and grabbed her by the elbow, leading her out of the cottage.

"Don't worry, Novus," he called over his shoulder to the half-fairy. "You don't have to come with us. I'll be back soon."

"Are you sure you don't want my assistance?" she asked, following to the door but staying back in the arch as the others exited.

"No," Amberly replied for Trace. "He's *fine*."

Once again, the five Defenders used the blue stone to teleport. This time, their destination was a short distance away from the late Albus's home to ask Gertrude where they could find the other Albus, or if she might be able to summon him for them. She greeted them warmly, pleased by their surprise visit, and invited them inside her home at once. Then, after they spoke with her, the sweet old woman wrote a quick note on a very small scroll of paper, rolled it up, tied it with a bow, and placed it around the ankle of a *three-headed* crow. She had summoned the... *thing* with a short, high-pitched whistle. When it appeared, all she needed to do was tell it who the message was for, and the bird took flight. Gertrude barely got through asking the teens if they wanted some tea before a loud whooshing noise sounded outside, and then Albus entered the magnificent tree trunk home.

The team had all been sitting around the table in the kitchen area, but they stood at his arrival. Something about this Albus's presence made it seem as though they shouldn't stay seated when he walked into a room.

He wore dark navy robes and a strange-looking velvet hat.

"I poofed over here the second I got the message, Gertrude. What brings you all here today?" he asked in his strong, commanding voice.

Kaos had hardly gotten to know the other Albus, but still, he was so different compared to the one before them. This Albus was so serious, so strict, so intimidating. The other Albus was a bit more... aloof.

He had a more carefree spirit about him. He was easier to talk to. Easier to ask questions to. They were more comfortable with him. Kaos couldn't speak for the others, but he got the feeling they were just as nervous in front of this Albus as he felt.

"Something happened," Kire said, being the one to speak up. Albus got a steely look in his dull-colored eyes and waited. "Rose is missing. We can't find her." His voice cracked as he spoke.

Slowly, Albus nodded his head as he processed it.

"We're hoping you can help us," Amberly said, piping up next. "If there's something you can do. If there's some way you can tell where she might be."

"We can't use Halo," Kaos added. "The book has to save energy until it's ready to give the warning about the battle starting. It's useless until then."

Albus motioned back to the table. "Why don't you all sit back down?"

"Can you help us or not?" Kire asked, refusing to do as Albus suggested while the other three moved to sit.

"Sit, Kire," Albus demanded.

Reluctantly, Kire finally obeyed and joined them around the table. Gertrude sat silently, watching the scene unfold before her.

"Now," Albus began, commanding the presence of the room. "I cannot tell you where Rose is."

Kaos felt his heart sink. It wasn't good news. Not only did they need Rose, but Kaos was *actually* worried about her. Wondering what happened. Where she went. Who could have taken her. Or did she run away?

"Great," Kire said, his voice dark and his attitude darker.

"But I *can* tell you this," Albus continued. All of their heads snapped up with a sense of hope as they waited. "She is still alive."

"She is?" Kire gasped out. "H-how—how would you know that?"

"I know because of your gifts. And *you* should know because of your gifts. If something had happened to Rose, you all would have felt it. You are all connected by those gifts in the physical, literal sense. *You* may not know it, but your bodies and your minds do. Your gifts would have shown you that part of the unity you all have was broken. Each in their own way."

"But what if they *have* done something, and we've just missed it?" Kire asked.

"Not possible," Albus said. "From all of the past fighters that failed, they recalled knowing without a doubt, even though they didn't have proof when another member of their team had passed."

"Whoa," Trace breathed out, his eyes widened in amazement.

"That's great news, Kire," Amberly told her brother, placing a hand on his shoulder and giving it a gentle squeeze.

For the first time since Rose went missing, Kire gave them all a shadow of a smile. The corners of his lips turned upward. His eyes didn't match it, but they at least had a new glimmer in them. A hopeful one.

"So... how can we go about finding her then?" Kaos asked. "Do you at least have any tips for us? Any ideas for where we should search? Any magical items we should retrieve and use to help us?"

"I am afraid that the advice I have to give you is not going to be all that helpful and reassuring," Albus replied, stroking his beard slowly and deliberately, looking grave.

"Why? What's your advice?" Amberly asked.

"My advice is that there's not much time left. But I'm sure you all know that. I suggest you do whatever you can to find Rose, whatever that means. And quickly. Because I fear without her, without the completed piece of your group, you don't stand a chance against Yash."

The advice from the *great and powerful* Albus had not been what Kaos wanted to hear. Not what *any* of them had wanted to hear. It felt more like a lecture than anything.

"Thanks, but we all could've told you that," Kaos barked at the old man, unable to keep quiet because he had grown so frustrated so quickly.

"We *have* been looking for her," Kire complained loudly, slamming a fist down on the tabletop. "So many people are out there looking for her! They say the first twenty-four hours are crucial, and it's been longer than that! It's great that she's still alive, but we don't have the first clue where she could be. What could've happened to her? We're not police officers. We're not detectives. If *they* can't find her, how are *we* supposed to?"

"This is horrible," Amberly said in a quiet voice, lowering her head. "We should've never let Rose out of our sight. We should all be sticking together at all times right now. We just don't know what's gonna happen at any point anymore. Times are too scary. Too unpredictable."

"There's no use talking about what we should have done," Kire snapped at her. "It doesn't help anything. What are we going to do? How are we going to find her?"

"We're all connected by our gifts, right?" Kaos tried. "We would know if she died. Our gifts would be able to tell us somehow. What if that also works for locating a member of the group? What if our powers give us some sense of direction if we just lean into them and listen?"

It sounded stupid to him even as he said it. But he had always thought the idea of magic being real was stupid before he became a Defender.

"Well, maybe *you* guys can do that, but I can't." Kire crossed his arms and leaned back in his seat. He was so defeated, so hopeless, so wrecked about this whole situation. Kaos had been told many times that love in high school was just puppy love and that it was impossible to compare to the *real* thing. But looking at Kire right then, Kaos could tell Kire loved her more than just puppy love. He could tell how real it was.

Albus cleared his throat, and everyone went silent. "I want to tell you all a story," he began.

"Do we even have time for that?" Kire interrupted.

"Perhaps not, but I do think it is a story you'll want to listen to. It's about the other Albus. About one of the last times I had an important conversation with him."

"About what?" Amberly asked.

"Why, about you. About the Defenders, of course."

"What did he say?" Kaos asked.

"Well, if you all stop asking me questions, I might be able to tell you."

The Defenders pursed their lips. Kaos used to say he couldn't care less about anything their Albus had to say. That he couldn't care less about Albus at all. He didn't like that this destiny had been thrown at him, and he didn't like that this old man with no clue about how their realm worked was trying to tell them how they needed to act and what they needed to do. But Kaos had since learned that it was all valuable information. That while Albus had seemed somewhat like a strange, senile old man nobody would take seriously in the Earth realm, Kaos now wanted to hang onto every word of this story.

"We were walking through a meadow together," Albus began. He had his hands clasped together on top of the table as he shot Gertrude a supportive glance as though to tell her she'd recognize this story. "I was helping him forage for ingredients for a certain procurement he needed. I knew that the Defenders were weighing heavily on his mind, that he couldn't stop thinking about them, even for a second, because, as you know, the Albuses are connected."

"That's right," Amberly recalled with a nod.

Albus continued. "I sensed something was weighing on him, so I invited him to talk about it. I asked him if everything was all right. And he told me that actually, everything *was* all right. Everything was surprisingly far better off than it had ever been. Because the newest group with the gifts had gotten further than anyone else had, and it was hard to believe because it was just a bunch of children."

The gang all looked around at each other, Kaos smirking at them triumphantly. Maybe they were children, but they could kick some serious alien and magical creature booty.

"So then I asked him what the problem was because I could tell *something* ailed him. And he told me he was restless. He told me it was giving Gertrude a hard time because she's always been so caring and so giving, and it was difficult for her to see Albus so stressed out."

Gertrude nodded. "You were all so important to him. I don't think you'll ever realize just how much."

"Maybe it's because we are kids," Trace suggested, giving a light shrug. "Maybe he worried about us more because he felt like he had some sort of responsibility over us, like a parent or a guardian."

"He was indeed your guardian," Albus said. "And you're on the right track, Trace. As I'm sure you all know, Albus and Gertrude lost the only son they ever had. Albus rarely liked to talk about him. But he did that day out on the meadow, to me. He told me that he suspected because he knew what it was like to be a father, he felt a peculiar closeness to you. And *because* he had lost his child, he felt a familiar worry of the same thing happening again."

"That's so sad," Amberly whispered.

Albus nodded in agreement. "I'll be frank—I asked him if he thought that even though you five had gotten this far, if he still lacked confidence that you would be able to defeat Yash."

Nobody in the room even breathed. Kaos certainly wanted to know what their Albus really thought of them. He wanted to know what the next words out of this Albus's mouth would be.

"He stopped walking and looked up at me with an expression so serious, so certain. And he said, 'I have the utmost belief in them. They might be young, but they are powerful. Their youth, their naivety, their lack of knowledge of how cruel the world can really be, I think all of that has aided them. I truly think they can do this. I truly think they have a shot at defeating Yash once and for all.'"

Kaos looked at the others to see them smiling. But Kaos was more surprised than anything. He had expected Albus to badmouth them, to say there wasn't a chance, that he was thinking about them so much only because he was planning how to revise his strategy for the next group of Defenders.

"So then... what had him so bothered?" Amberly asked.

"Your suffering," Albus replied. "It made him sad to think about all the things you had to do. All the things you still had yet to do. He said your youth would be stripped away from you because of all of this. He hated that, as kids, you should be off enjoying your lives, but instead, you had a larger responsibility than even any grown adult ever had."

The corners of Kaos's lips turned downward as he thought about it. When was the last time he had had some real fun? When was the last time he had gotten to act like a normal teenager? It wasn't like he would get another chance. This was it. This was all he had. Adulthood was just around the corner. Kaos no longer felt like he could be a kid.

"Wow," Trace muttered. When Kaos looked over at him, he saw that Trace was eyeing Gertrude. "You're completely right," he told her. "I had no idea how much he cared."

"Well, now you should have a better sense," she replied, her voice airy and her eyes shining.

"I just can't get over that he actually thought we could do this," Kaos pointed out. This got a chuckle out of everyone. It eased the tension a little.

"He did. And because of that," Albus said, "I think you can, too. Just like I think you can find Rose. It might seem hopeless, it might seem impossible, but look at what you've done so far. Everything that's happened should be all you need to feel assured that anything is possible, that anything is achievable. And looking back at the massive battle you fought here in our realm, at how well you all worked together then, you should all know what you need to do in order to feel that strength again."

"Starting with finding Rose," Kire said.

"But also, working on your inner selves," Albus said.

The room grew quiet as Albus stared at each one of them individually. His eyes landed on Kaos last.

"I know my friend told you there was a darkness inside of you. I know you didn't like to hear it. But I wanted to check in on that. Do you still feel that darkness inside of you?"

"I never did to begin with," Kaos said. Maybe he was in denial. Maybe he didn't want to accept it.

"I think you need to have some accountability," Amberly suggested, looking hesitant as though she were worried Kaos was going to react badly to her comment. "You never own up to your mistakes, Kaos. It's like you can't even see that the things you do affect those around you. And not in a good way."

"Give me one good example," Kaos dared. When had *he* ever messed up?

Aside from letting Rezin into his head.

Aside from breaking up Trace and Amberly.

Aside from making Rose cry more than once.

"You don't use your powers for good," Amberly pointed out. "I don't need a specific example. There are so many of them."

Oh yeah—and aside from Kaos using his crown to make everyone bend to his will.

"Okay..." he trailed off, trying to find a way to remedy all of it. But I haven't done anything bad in a while. I'm not—I'm not dark. I'm not evil. I'm trying to save the world. I mean, *come* on—how can I be *so* 'dark' if I'm trying to save lives?"

"Maybe you're healing from your darkness," Albus suggested. "The more healing you all do individually and together as a team, the more successful you will be. Don't ignore the way that you're feeling. Don't ignore your actions. And don't act without thinking. Don't act without feeling." He sighed and pushed his chair back, getting to his feet. "Alas, you don't need me to tell you all of this. You already know what you need to do. I have to get back; I was in the middle of figuring out an important equation, and I must get back to it before my focus dissipates. So with that, I will be leaving you now."

When the group walked out of Gertrude's house together, they all talked animatedly, putting their heads together and focusing hard on how they might find Rose. Kaos knew it was Albus who had reinvigorated them. He had rejuvenated their spirits. He had given them some confidence by reassuring them that he knew they could do this. And it helped to know that Rose was still alive out there and that they would all know if she no longer was.

"So..." Amberly trailed off as they walked down a path covered in fallen leaves, little pebbles, and strange weeds growing out of the ground. They were almost neon yellow, and the tips of their blades split off into five smaller blades that then connected to each other.

There were tons of foliage there in the Albus realm that didn't exist in their world, like the magical beings... and *magic* in general.

"What is it?" Kire asked her eagerly. "Do you have an idea? Let's hear it. I don't care if you think it will sound stupid. Remember what Albus said. We need to do everything we can."

"No, I know," Amberly told him. "It's not about that. But it is about something our Albus said."

"Okay..." Kire clearly didn't like getting off the subject of finding the missing member of their group.

"He's right," Amberly said. "Our Albus is right about what he told the other Albus. Our youth *was* stripped from us, and it *does* suck. But... it is what it is, and there's nothing we can change about that, ya know? We are older because of this, even if technically we're staying the same exact age since we've suddenly become immortal... Anyway, the fact of the matter is, everything we've been fighting over, everything that's prevented us from being the team we need to be, it's all so insignificant, so stupid, in the grand scheme of things. None of that is important. What is important is finding Rose. Finding Rose and then defeating Yash. Saving the world. That's a huge responsibility. Who cares who did what, who said what, and who broke up who? If we're all dead, none of it is going to matter anyway, so it shouldn't matter now. I am over everything. And I'm sorry for the way I've behaved. I finally feel that I'm at a point where I am open and accepting of all of you, of all of us as a group. I am... I'm letting go of all of it. For Rose. For the world."

Kaos was almost dumbfounded by her monologue. He would've never in a million years pictured Amberly saying anything like this to anyone. He had never seen her be so accepting. He'd never seen her show so much grace. He'd never seen her be more mature than she was being right now. Amberly before never knew how to rise above it all. None of them really did, he supposed. But everything she said, she was so right. *None of it matters.*

"Yeah," Trace said, speaking first, even though Kaos had just opened his mouth to do so. "It's all so stupid. I'm over it, too." He glanced at Kaos, who nodded quickly in agreement.

"Same here. I want us to be the best we can be. I've always wanted that. I've always wanted us to be as powerful as possible. Not only because it'll help us win, but because it feels *freaking* good." He smirked at them.

"Wow," Kire said, looking around at all of them. "I don't even recognize you three anymore. Where are those bullies who chased me through the woods?"

Playfully, they all shoved him.

And as they all smiled around at each other, something shifted. Kaos didn't have his crown on, but he could still feel it. As Amberly let out a small gasp, staring at her gauntlet, while Trace and Kire snapped their heads up to look at each other, Kaos knew they could feel it, too. It was as though something was glowing right in his middle, brighter and brighter. He felt strong.

He felt ready.

14

The group of teenagers could have all taken the magical stone and popped right back to the portal that would lead them into their realm, but instead of doing so, they walked. It was as though none of them wanted to leave and go back to face what might be waiting. Any second they could stay here, they held onto. As they walked, Amberly placed herself beside Kire ahead of Kaos and Trace, comforting him and saying reassuring things to him about how she felt confident they were going to find Rose and that everything was going to be okay.

Who is *this chick?*

It left Kaos and Trace walking beside each other, awkwardly silent. Kaos figured he should probably say something—after all, they had all agreed they were over it, right? They could stop hating each other finally?

"Do you ever think the Albuses all get together and have competitions on who has the best beard?" he asked Trace, breaking the silence between them.

Trace chuckled, his mouth spreading into a grin. "Definitely."

"I know I haven't seen the other Albuses closely, but I think *our* Al would win. I don't know about that Albus back there, though—

his looked a little short." It was silly to say because while the new Albus's beard *was* shorter than their Albus's, *this* Albus's beard was still longer than any Kaos had seen in his realm. The beard went almost down to Albus's navel.

Do Albuses even have *navels?*

Trace joined in on the teasing of the second Albus. "And what do you think happened to him that made him have the stick up his butt? He is so much more serious than the other Albus was."

Kaos laughed. "*So* serious!"

It felt good to be talking to his old friend again like this. Good, but it was still weird. Kaos could still sense the rift between the two of them. He knew the relationship would never go back to what it was before. He wasn't certain that they could ever go back to being *best* friends again. Not after what Kaos had done. Not after the stunt he regretted greatly. The one he regretted even more so now, now that he had been forgiven. He didn't deserve their forgiveness. He realized now that what he had done was truly horrible. He knew what it took to be a good person, and he had never been one in his life. But that could change.

"I'm so glad that my girlfriend being missing is humorous to you," Kire threw over his shoulder at the other two. Amberly turned him back around and forced him to keep walking.

"Just ignore them, Kire. I'm sure they're still worried about finding Rose. They're just having a... moment."

"Don't make it so weird," Trace called to her. She briefly stuck her tongue out at him. Then she smiled at Kaos.

When was the last time I got a smile from Amberly?

Suddenly, Kaos felt like a million bucks, which was strange because they were still in a terrible situation.

"So..." Kaos continued talking to Trace as Kire and Amberly dove into their own separate conversation. "What's it like staying here in this realm?" He had been dying to know.

"I really like it, man," Trace said. "Novus is great. The towns-people are great. With all of the drama in my life left behind, with a bunch of people around me who have no idea who I am or where I came from, it feels good. It's nice to forget every once in a while. You know? Here, I can just be the hero, the person they look up to, the person they need. And it's easy. A lot easier than being home."

"I get it," Kaos said. "And you've really been staying at Novus's place this whole time?"

"Yeah." Trace had a sheepish expression on his face.

"What's that look for?" Kaos asked him, noticing it.

"Mom would *kill* me if she knew I've been having sleepovers with a girl." He said it quietly so that Amberly couldn't hear. "But it's not even anything like *that*," he added. "Still, if I tried to tell my mom that, she wouldn't listen at all."

"But you guys have become pretty good friends?"

"Yeah, she's cool. It's hilarious because she wants to visit our realm, but I tried to explain to her that it's not worth seeing. That this place is way more exciting. She doesn't believe me."

"It's hard to picture anyone being excited about visiting a place like Earth when they have literal magic where they live."

"Exactly. Actually, it was kind of weird. I was going to bring her to our realm. I told her we could go check it out but that I didn't want to stay long, and that I didn't want to see anyone. I was ready to go and everything. But then she suddenly changed her mind. Makes me think she just pretended like she wanted to go to be nice or something. I don't know. Chicks are confusing."

"You got that right." Kaos stared at Amberly as he said it.

"But I don't know," Trace said with a shrug. "I have been thinking about it a lot. About going back. About you guys. About everything going down. I've been feeling responsible. Guilty, I guess."

"Good, you *should* feel guilty. Because we've needed you. And your mom *definitely* needs you."

"Don't you think that as her child, *I* should be the one needing her?"

"Yeah... I guess that's true. So then... if you stay here, what are you gonna do?"

"What do you mean?" Trace asked.

"Are you gonna live with Novus forever? Or are you going to eventually get yourself your own place? *Build* yourself your own place? Are you really going to be a knight?"

"I don't know." Trace rubbed the back of his neck. "I've sort of just been living in the 'here and now,' you know what I mean?"

"Huh." Kaos snuck a look at Trace, trying to figure out how he felt about Novus. If he maybe had feelings for her. And if he *did* have feelings for her, what did that mean about his feelings for Amberly? It was hard to tell. Kaos was terrible at that kind of thing. He himself could never even tell if a girl liked him.

In front of them, Amberly and Kire stopped walking when they reached a fork in the road. They turned around and eyed Trace.

"What?" Trace asked them. "Why'd we stop?"

"I think... I think this is where we part... If that's what is going to happen," Amberly said slowly. Nervously.

Trace looked at the two separate roads. One leading back to Novus's village. The other one leading back to the portal.

"Oh," he said, as though he hadn't realized the time to decide had come already.

"You *still* want to stay here?" Kire asked.

"I know it may seem like this realm needs you, but your home needs you more," Amberly said. Her eyes dug into Trace as though she were searching for his soul.

"I don't know, guys," Trace said, walking over to a large boulder and collapsing down on it as though exhausted. "I like it here."

"*Really*?" Amberly asked, squinting. "Do they even have indoor plumbing?"

"They have magic."

"Touché."

"Come on, Trace. We need to put everybody's heads together if we're going to find Rose," Kire said. "And Amberly is right about what she said earlier. She's actually been right about a lot of things today, which is weird."

Amberly slapped him on the shoulder.

Kire continued. "But we really do all need to stick together right now. Everything is so unpredictable. When Halo finally gives the warning that Yash is coming, how much planning time is going to come with that warning?"

"Yeah," Amberly said, "What if you're here, and Yash strikes? What if we're so busy fighting him and trying to be the Defenders of the Earth realm that we can't get to you to tell you to help us?"

"Look," Trace started, "I get what you all are saying, but there are a lot of benefits to me staying here, too. The army, for example. All of those villagers that want to help us. That are willing to come to our world to protect it as we have protected theirs."

"It's not like you can't come back here ever," Kaos said. "Periodically, sure. You can return, and you can train them and get them prepared and whatever. I don't really know how one would prepare for the end of the world, but that's just my two cents about it."

"And I know you're upset with your mom," Amberly continued. "But she's actually been doing really well."

"The last time she drank was when the sinkhole happened. She said it was a slipup. That she hasn't had one since," Kaos told him. "She actually wanted us to tell you that."

"Yeah, because we went and reassured her that you're okay so that she wasn't beside herself with worry," Amberly added.

Trace refused to look at any of them, and he also refused to reply.

"At the end of the day, it's your decision, man," Kaos said, "but I think you know what the right thing to do is here."

"Staying here would just be selfish," Amberly argued.

"Everyone is selfish," Trace told her. "To an extent. People don't generally make all of their decisions based on what other people want. They make their decisions based on what *they* want. You could say it's selfish that you want me back in the other realm. You don't care that I'm suffering. You don't care what I want to do. You are only thinking of yourselves. Am I right?"

"Dude... we're thinking about the human race, actually," Kire interjected. "You know, the one we're supposed to be saving?"

"I get that. I'm just saying. There's always something in it for everyone. 'Selfish' is a stupid word."

"Oh my God, *fine*," Amberly groaned. "What else do you want me to say? Do you want us to beg? Do you want us on our hands and knees, Trace? Because we need you to come back. Kaos can say it's up to you and it's your decision and whatever, but he's only acting like he doesn't care. He wants you to come back, too. Everyone does."

Trace was still uncertain. "I just..."

"What?" Amberly asked him, her hands on her hips. "What do you want, Trace?"

"I've changed," he replied. "A lot. I am not the same person I was at the beginning of the school year. That guy? The one who antagonized people, got in trouble, and fought people for money? I don't want to be that guy anymore. I'm not that guy. I don't want to be a bully. I don't want to be some sort of lackey to Kaos."

"You make it out like I forced you into being the way you were," Kaos snapped. "I never forced you into doing anything."

"I know, I know." Trace hung his head. "I like helping people. I like being the good guy. Being a Defender has taught me that."

"Consider yourself a saint, then," Amberly said impatiently. "Consider *all* of us saints. We're the good guys now. Until the end of time. Okay? Can you please just come back with us?"

"I want my mom to stop drinking."

"I really think she has," Amberly said.

"She'd rather stop drinking than lose you, that's for sure," Kaos replied. "That woman cares about you more than anything."

Trace let out a long, uneasy sigh. He ran his hand through his hair, sneaking glances around at everyone. They all waited, some more patiently than others.

"What's it gonna be, Trace?" Amberly demanded. "We can't stand here forever and wait for you to answer. You're either coming, or you're not. No, scratch that. You're either coming, or we are *dragging* your back."

"Speak for yourself," Kaos said, holding his hands up and stepping away. "I'm not gonna force him to do anything."

"I..." Trace trailed off and continued to keep them all waiting. Then, finally, when it looked like Amberly's head was about to explode, he let out a sly smile and looked up at them. "I guess I *have* been really wanting to get a haircut."

15

"**I** hope you boys are ready for an all-nighter," Amberly said when they returned to their realm and neared the mouth of the cave. "We have some Rose-searching to do, and to start off, we need to search this forest."

They stopped just outside of it, and Kire, Trace, and Kaos nodded at Amberly in agreement. Kaos had no trouble letting Amberly take the lead on this one; his thoughts were a bit scattered. Everything that had happened in the Albus realm earlier replayed in his mind.

"What do we tell our parents?" Kire asked.

"A lie, of course," she said, tossing her hair back. "Everyone text their parents that they're staying at one of our houses for the night. Don't let them say no, either. Don't pose it like a question. It's a statement, and if they want to punish us, they'll have to do it later."

Kaos hesitated, only because he didn't think he needed to bother with the text message to his parents when he could just use his crown on them when he came home to make them believe that he had never been gone in the first place. But then he remembered what he had discussed with the others before. Kaos wasn't a dark person, and he needed to stop messing with people's free will just to benefit himself. So he did as Amberly instructed and sent his mom a text.

"What's next?" Kire asked. It was a strange sight to see him patiently waiting to be told what to do by his former arch-nemesis.

"Okay, so... now..." She looked around, scanning their surroundings while she thought about it. "I know I said that we needed to stick together, but now I'm saying we need to split up. We'll spread out and only search in half-mile increments in opposite directions, then we'll reconvene, move to a new location, and repeat the strategy."

"What if we don't find her?" Kire asked. "Where do we search next?"

"We'll have to get to that if and when it comes, Kire. Just focus on right now, okay? If you think too far ahead, you're going to lose sight of our current objective. I need you to focus on *now*."

"That's what you gotta do," Trace agreed. "It's like I told Kaos a little while ago. We have to live in the 'here and now.' Thinking ahead? It's too freaky."

"Fine, okay." Kire sounded resigned. "Just don't forget that I basically have no magical abilities right now. Nothing to protect me out here. No shield."

"Just yell if you need us," Amberly said. "Like I said, don't go further than half a mile, and then come right back here."

It didn't matter that Kaos was tired and hungry. It didn't matter how unprepared he was to pull a sudden all-nighter forest search for their missing member. He had heard the new Albus loud and clear—they needed to find Rose, and that came before anything else.

His stomach growled loudly.

That includes eating, I guess.

When the group split up, Kaos headed back into the mouth of the cave, wanting to retrace their steps and search other parts. Rose liked it in places like this, doing her little science projects. What if Yash did something that scared her, and she was just hiding out in here? She might've made herself a pretty nice hideout with her plant-manipulating abilities.

Now alone with his thoughts, he recalled what Trace had told him in the Albus realm earlier, about Novus. Kaos got stuck on something when he recalled it, on how Novus talked about wanting to go to the Earth realm but then suddenly changed her mind when Trace tried to take her. What was up with that? Why did it feel so strange to Kaos? Sure, it could be like Trace said, and she could've just been pretending to want to go to the Earth realm to be nice, but Kaos still couldn't shake the feeling that maybe it was something else, something he wanted to look into. Something he *needed* to look into, fast.

There was no time to go back and wait for the others. He didn't want to be yelled at by Kire for straying from the mission. He didn't want to be forced to stay. But he also had no phone service to let the others know he wouldn't be returning. So, knowing they'd be looking for him, he used a rock to carve his note in huge letters into the dirt:

I'LL BE RIGHT BACK!

It would have to do. Kaos had to follow this hunch, and there was no time to lose.

KAOS FELT MORE powerful than he'd ever been. When he placed the crown on his head again after the earlier pain, it felt completely different. It was as though he had removed a part of himself, like a snowman losing its nose. And he wasn't a whole, complete being until he had that crown back on.

As he walked through the Albus realm by himself, his body hummed as if it were a piece of electrical equipment. He felt unstoppable. The last time the quintets had worked well together in battle in this realm, Kaos still hadn't fully gotten the hang of his gift yet. So, while the team had been stronger *together* individually, Kaos had felt weak. It was a totally different story now. He felt strong even without the others there with him. He felt the camaraderie as though they were right behind him. He even tried his own idea; he stood very still, closed his eyes, and willed his crown to lead him in the direction of Rose. It didn't work, but hope was not lost, not yet.

It felt weird to be at Novus's house alone. As he walked up the path to the front door, he sensed something in the air. He couldn't put his finger on it, but something seemed as though it had changed since they were here earlier.

Surprise stretched across Novus's face when she answered the door.

"Hey, sorry—me again," Kaos said awkwardly, giving her a small wave before shoving his hands in his pockets.

"Kaos?" Novus stepped outside and looked around, as if searching for the others.

"It's just me," Kaos told her. What she *didn't* know was that he was already using the crown, or at least... he was *trying* to.

What is happening?

Novus was right there in front of him, and yet, Kaos couldn't get a read on her thoughts with his crown. How was that possible?

"Is everything okay?" she asked.

"I lost the others," he said. "After we left Albus's, I stopped to tie my shoe, thinking they all saw me and were waiting just up ahead, but when I looked up, they were out of sight."

"They left you behind?"

"It was probably on accident. They were in a deep discussion about something."

"Well, I'm sure they'll come back here, right? Or at least, won't Trace? You won't be lost for long."

"Yeah, that's what I was hoping—that if I just came here, they'll eventually get back to me."

He kept trying to see inside her mind, but still, he got nothing. Just a stone wall. Not even a whisper of a thought. But how could that be when he felt so aligned with the crown? So powerful? When he felt more in tune with his gift than ever?

"Good thinking," Novus said. "Um... are you all right?"

"Huh?"

She crinkled her nose. "You look like you ate something bad."

Kaos realized he was twisting his face in concentration as he tried to figure out why his crown wasn't working. "Oh," he said, relaxing it. "Yeah, I'm fine. Just worried about the others."

"Right. Well, why don't you come in and wait for them?"

Did their gifts not work on half-fairies? No, that couldn't be it, or else he wouldn't have been able to use his gifts on all those minions that they had defeated.

"Thank you so much," Kaos said, following her into the small cottage. Something was different about the interior from the way it had been this morning. His eyes went to the table, where he saw a spread of tiny vials, all filled with different kinds of liquids. In the center of the table was a cauldron, and surrounding it were ingredients that didn't look familiar. What was she working on?

"Sorry about the mess," she said, giving him an embarrassed look. "I figured since it's been so long since you guys left that maybe we weren't coming back."

"Don't worry about it," Kaos said, wanting to keep the conversation flowing easily. He didn't want to make things weird by letting her know Trace had no intentions of staying, that he was already back in their world, waiting for Kaos to return.

When she looked at him, he nodded toward the mess on the table.

"What exactly are you working on over here?"

She pursed her bottom lip, her right eye twitching as she fixed her gaze quickly to her feet. "I don't know exactly. Just testing out some new things."

"I see. Cool."

She obviously didn't want to tell him exactly what it was she was making, but her silence and sudden shiftiness told Kaos all he needed to know. She had concocted something. She knew about his gift, about what he could do, and it seemed she'd made an elixir to prevent Kaos from being able to see inside her mind, from being able to read her thoughts. Why would she do that? What did she have to hide?

He turned his focus to the other part of his gift, the part that could make people do things. As Novus moved to pour some hot water into a glass, he concentrated on making her release the glass from her left hand. She did so, and it shattered when it hit the ground.

"Oh my goodness, I'm so clumsy!" She gasped. "I'll go get a broom."

She scurried away.

That's odd, Kaos thought. He hadn't been hopeful that it would work, but he could still control her. He could make her do what he wanted. Apparently, that wasn't as important to Novus as hiding her thoughts from him. Either that or she just didn't know about this part of the gift.

When she returned, she got down to begin sweeping.

Kaos forced her to stop.

She looked confused and stared down at hands that suddenly refused to cooperate.

He made her stand up.

She let out another gasp of surprise. "What's happening?"

"Must be a reaction to one of your concoctions," Kaos suggested with a shrug.

She looked at him sharply. "*You're* doing this."

He shrugged again. Then he walked over to her front door and held it open for her. "After you."

"What are you talking about? I'm not going anywhere."

"We'll see about that."

He forced her to move.

She tried to resist, but there was nothing that could be done. Making someone do what he wanted had never been easier. He was so glad that he had made up with the others earlier so that this would work so well.

"Stop," Novus tried. "What are you doing to me? I don't want to go anywhere."

She went outside anyway, and Kaos followed her. He kept her in front of him, having her lead the way as they started to make their journey to her carriage and Pegasus.

From there, they soared through the sky, and Kaos was able to take a breather on the mind control because what was Novus going to do? Jump out of a flying carriage?

Instead, he looked out the window, still finding it incredible to be magically transported this way. If only it took magic and not technology to make things fly in his world.

"Where are we going?" Novus snapped. "You weren't lost at all, were you?"

He pointed at her. "Smart girl."

"I don't understand what's going on."

"No? And yet, you created an elixir to prevent me from being able to read your mind."

"Who told you that?"

She asked it so sharply that her eyes narrowed, and it made Kaos laugh. "Nobody told me that. I figured it out for myself! And you've just confirmed it by reacting like that."

"Where. Are. We. Going?" she seethed.

"To the portal. I'm sorry, Novus; I know you told Trace that you didn't want to go. But we need you in our realm. Trace specifically needs you. He went back already. But then something happened. I don't know exactly how Trace thinks you can help him, but he told me it was an emergency and that I had to get you there no matter what."

"But I... I can't go. I... I was in the middle of something when you rudely interrupted. You have to bring me back. Trace will be fine."

The Pegasus began to descend. Kaos straightened his crown, ready to keep manipulating Novus.

"Don't do it," she demanded.

Kaos cackled. "Like I would listen to any of your demands over my best friend's request. He knows I have his back."

"I can't just up and go to your realm, Kaos. Time works differently there. It would screw things up for me here when I got back. I-I have duties. Obligations."

"Yes, you do, and one of those obligations is getting to Trace and helping him, like he requested. It's not a big deal, Novus. It's not going to take long."

She nervously chewed on her bottom lip again.

When the carriage landed, he had to force her out of it.

"Please stop," she kept begging. "I can't go, Kaos. I can't do this right now. You have to let me go back."

But he kept forcing her to make her way to the glowing blue arch. "I don't get what you're so freaked out about," he said. "Did Trace really make our realm seem *that* bad?"

"It's not that."

"Then what is it?"

Novus was only steps from it now. Kaos manipulated her into going through it. And yet, she didn't. Her body would not move into the glowing blue mist. Her feet stayed planted firmly on the ground.

"Oh, Novus," Kaos said, making a *tsk*-ing noise and slowly shaking his head at her. "I was afraid of this."

Kaos had been right in his suspicions. Whether or not Novus wanted to go into the Earth realm, she couldn't. The portal would not let her enter. Because it only allowed the good to travel through it.

Novus was evil.

But now the question was: what had she done?

16

Upon Kaos's return to the Earth realm, after he abandoned Novus and hurried back, his phone started working again. Even though it still didn't have service, he could see the time. Only thirty seconds had disappeared while he was away. He hadn't even needed to make that note in the dirt.

He retraced his steps and met up with the others once more back at the mouth of the cave where they had first separated. He was the last to get back.

But probably only by thirty seconds, he told himself.

"You guys," Kaos said before any of them could start freaking out about how they still hadn't found Rose. "I went back to the Albus realm to see Novus."

"You *what*?" Trace asked, his eyebrows raised sky-high.

"Why?" Amberly asked next.

"I had to follow a hunch I was having," Kaos admitted. "And it turns out I was right."

"What are you talking about?" Trace asked.

"About what?" Kire asked.

"Trace," Kaos began, "Novus isn't who you think she is."

"Who is she?" he asked. "And who do you think I think she is?"

"Wait, what?" Amberly asked with a puzzled look.

"When I got to her place," Kaos explained, "she had obviously been concocting something like some sort of witch. Trace, are you *sure* she's a half-fairy?"

"I don't have any reason to not believe her," he replied.

"Well, anyway, I tried to use my crown on her to see into her mind, to see if she had any secrets, anything she was hiding. And guess what? It didn't work. I was blocked because of some concoction she whipped up. I'm sure of it."

"Why would she do that?" Amberly asked.

"I'm getting to that." Kaos couldn't get the words out quickly enough, but he wanted to make sure the others fully understood what had happened. "The thing is, Trace, did Novus know that my powers could also control people and make them do things?"

"I don't know. I think so. I think everyone knows what our gifts do in that realm. Stories of our battle are everyone's favorite thing to tell at get-togethers."

"Maybe she just hadn't finished that potion," Kaos said, just thinking aloud.

"Finished what potion? What's going on? Do fairies even make potions?" Trace asked.

"I was able to make her do things still," Kaos informed them. "So I took her to the portal. It was weird what you said to me about her, Trace—how she seemed all gung-ho about going to the Earth realm but then changed her mind when it became a reality."

"Wait! Are you saying Novus couldn't get through the portal?!" Kire asked, jumping to the conclusion and figuring it out before anyone else.

"Exactly," Kaos said.

"Hang on a sec..." The gears turned a little slower in Amberly's head. "So then... She's a traitor. She's not good; she's... evil!"

"Yep," Kaos said.

Trace was completely bewildered. "Evil?"

"Is it so hard to believe?" Amberly asked him. "I know for sure *I* didn't get a good vibe from her."

"Well, *yeah*, but that's just because you didn't like that I was talking to her," Trace pointed out.

Amberly's expression turned sour.

"Wait a second," Kire interrupted their quarrel, his voice suddenly loud and commanding. Everyone turned their heads to him. "You don't think... You don't think Novus could have Rose, do you?"

"Oh my God," Amberly gasped. "She has Rose!"

"Guys, let's just think about this for a second," Trace tried. "Why would she help us, give us money, and give me a place to stay, but then kidnap Rose? What need does she have for her?"

"Who cares about her motive?" Kaos said. "Did you hear me? I tried to make her go through the portal, and she couldn't, Trace. You know what that means. It speaks for itself. It's a fact that Novus isn't one of the good guys."

"It just doesn't make any sense." Trace was crushed by the news. The betrayal was written all over his darkened expression.

"What on *Earth* are we still doing here?!" Kire barked, turning on his heel and taking off in a quick run back inside the cave.

"What is he doing?" Amberly said with a tired sigh. "We don't even have a plan yet!"

"We do," Kaos disagreed. "The plan is to follow him. Come on!"

The other three charged after him, and Kaos was more than willing to follow Kire's lead this time. He was excited, even, for the opportunity to catch Novus with her evil plot, to have that confrontation with her, to knock her off her high horse. They would get Rose back, and they wouldn't let any of her stupid fairy magic stop them from making that happen.

AFTER THEY ALL dove back through the portal and returned to the Albus realm, Kire whipped out the stone to teleport them to Novus's village. Before the others could put their hands on the rock, Amberly sternly placed a hand on Kire's shoulder.

"What exactly do you expect us to do once we get to her?" she asked. "Think about this, Kire. What is the plan? Are we just going to march in there and kill her? I know you're angry. I know you're anxious. I know you're ready to get Rose back. We all are. But we can't just barge in. What are we going to do?"

"If I have to kill her, if that's what it takes, I'm prepared to do it," Kire replied, holding his head up high. "You don't understand, Amberly. I will do whatever it takes. Whatever it takes."

"So you're going to kill her? When? Before she can even tell us where she's keeping Rose? This is just Kaos's theory anyway; we don't know for sure that she really did kidnap Rose!" Amberly said.

Kaos was impressed to see Amberly even bothering to try to reason with Kire right now, to try to make him see some sense in the situation, to think with rationality. Kire was smart. He had a good head on his shoulders. Overall, he was a good person. But when it came to Rose, there was a switch in him that flipped. All his morals, all his rationality, and all of his thinking flew out the window.

"Amberly!" Kire yelled, sick of the sisterly advice. "Put your hand on the dang rock!"

"Kire..." she trailed off, still looking unsure.

They really are siblings, Kaos thought to himself as he watched them interact.

Holding the teleportation stone out in the center of their circle, Kire shook it violently at Amberly. Kaos was fine with Kire's plan to just wing it and see what happened once they got to Novus, so he placed a hand on the rock, preventing Kire from being able to keep shaking it at Amberly. The others joined in, touching the rock and getting ready to teleport. Amberly was the only one still hesitant.

"I will leave you here," Kire barked, and Kaos believed him. Like Kire said—he would do anything to get Rose back.

Scoffing, Amberly reluctantly touched the stone at last, and the gang teleported right in front of Novus's cottage. There was no need to distance themselves from her home first and sneak up on her; they all had a plan to not have a plan. So, barging in was the best course of action.

Kaos ran after Kire, alongside Amberly and Trace, up the path to Novus's door. Kire burst through it, and they all crammed themselves inside the small space. Kaos wasn't certain what he would find waiting for them inside, but he hadn't been expecting Novus to be standing in her kitchen, glowering at all of them, her fists balled, ready for a fight, as though she had been waiting for them.

"Where is she?" Kire didn't waste any time.

"Where is who?" Novus asked, her voice completely different from the last time any of them had talked to her. She sounded purely wicked now.

"You know exactly who I'm talking about!" Kire raged.

"Come on, Novus, I told them everything," Kaos added. "I know Rose is here somewhere. I know you're hiding her. I know why you can't get through that portal."

"I knew you'd be back," she growled at him. "You're smart, Kaos. I learned that from your best friend."

"I don't have time to sit here and talk about this!" Kire barked.

"You better let her go, you wench," Amberly snarled.

Out of all the things any of them could've said, Amberly's insult seemed to anger Novus the most.

"*Wench*?!"

The half-fairy picked up an elixir of some dark blue liquid inside a vial, throwing it at them. They all ducked in cover as it shattered on the ground, and the dark blue liquid turned into a thick smoke.

"Get her!" Kire shouted, even though they could hardly see.

Amberly lifted the dining chair nearest her in the air with her telekinetic abilities and sent it flying through the smoke toward where Novus had last been standing. It crashed into the wall, unsuccessfully hitting her target. They choked and sputtered on the smoke around them. Kaos tried to listen to her thoughts in case maybe the potion had worn off since he was last there, but he still couldn't make anything out.

Trace lit his sword, allowing them to see right through the smoke. Novus was at her kitchen stove, preparing another concoction.

"I don't think so," Kire called, running at her. It didn't appear to matter to him that he didn't have an actual magical ability other than Halo's shield, which wouldn't work right now anyway. It didn't matter that he was running headfirst at an evil fairy with magical potions. Kaos practically rolled his eyes at the scene of it, thinking Kire was behaving recklessly. Then he ran after him to intervene.

Novus threw a concoction at Kire's feet as he approached her, and a magical rope appeared out of thin air, wrapping itself tightly around him, pinning him against the floor, unable to do anything but wiggle around in frustration.

"Why did you take her?!" he yelled at her instead of fighting. "What did she do to you, huh?"

She held up another vial. This time, Kaos used his mind control to make her drop it at her own feet. She cried out in both pain and anger as a giant mound of snow completely covered her body, forming like an overly soapy bubble bath from the dropped liquid on the ground.

"What are these things?!" Trace yelled about the elixirs. "Why are you doing this, Novus? I thought we were friends!"

"I told you not to trust her!" Amberly called to him, deciding *now* was the time to bring it up.

"I could never be friends with any of you," Novus hissed as she brushed the snow off herself, "not after what you did!"

"We didn't do anything!" Kaos replied. "Especially Rose. Rose wouldn't hurt a fly."

"Oh yeah? Then tell me, why is my mother dead?"

Free of the snow, Novus raced over to her table.

"Trace, fireball!" Kaos ordered. Catching on quicker than Kaos had ever seen his friend catch onto anything in his life, Trace used his sword, aiming it at the table with all of her other magical mixtures and concoctions, and a fireball flew out of the tip of it, whizzing past Kaos's head and crashing into the table, causing an explosion, destroying all of the concoctions in a fiery burst.

"No!" Novus roared.

"I don't understand!" Trace yelled at her. There was something hurt in his voice, like he didn't want to destroy her belongings, like he didn't want to be doing this to her. But he knew he had to. He knew he had no choice, and he would protect the other Defenders over Novus any day. "Why are you doing this?"

"I lied about what I said before!" she growled, dodging another flying object from Amberly. "I just wanted to gain your trust."

"Lied about what?" Kaos demanded.

"About how my mother died!"

"Wait a second," Trace said, growing still as he realized something. "When I first met you... that day at the cemetery when I was visiting Albus's grave..."

"Finally catching on now, are we?" she asked, sneering at him.

Betrayal was plain on Trace's face. "It wasn't a coincidence that we were both there at the same time," he deduced.

"How are you *just* this moment finally figuring it out?" she growled rhetorically.

Trace's betrayal changed to anger. "You'd been following me, watching me. Watching *us*. Plotting."

"I'm surprised that *you* would be the first to realize it, Trace," Novus hissed wickedly, "all things considered when it comes to *your* wit."

"What?" Amberly asked, "Realizing *what*?"

"Get me out of this!" Kire shouted, still tangled in the magical rope. "Get me out of this so I can kill her! Where is Rose?"

At this point, Kaos put the pieces together, too. Since Trace temporarily looked too angry to explain it to Amberly, Kaos took the lead. "During the battle," he announced, disregarding Kire and staying on topic with Novus. "The battle that we fought trying to protect this realm. Your mother was killed in the crossfire, wasn't she?"

Kire stopped wiggling and shouting for justice for a single moment, acknowledging and realizing what must have happened. Why Novus was so infuriated with them. Novus was simply getting her revenge.

"You destroyed so much on your oh-so-heroic journey to save our world!" Novus raged on. "You destroyed whatever you could in the process, caring about little else besides yourselves."

"Is she joking?" Amberly asked. "She has to be joking, right? Hello, dingbat?! We were risking our butts trying to protect your world! Explain to me how that makes us selfish."

"My mother was a healing fairy! She worked tirelessly, and on dangerous grounds, to provide aid to the wounded. And now, my mother is dead!"

As Novus unexpectedly rose into the air, Kaos didn't know why he hadn't predicted it happening sooner. Novus was a fairy, after all, wings and all, even though most of the time, they were concealed. It was easy for Kaos to forget she wasn't just a pretty, potion-wielding girl. None of the quintets could fly. This gave her an edge. And an advantage.

It was a shame that it was Rose who Novus decided to kidnap in retaliation. Were Rose there now, she would be the one to apologize to Novus. To explain how completely and totally sorry they were for the harm they caused when all they were trying to do was protect everyone. None of them wanted to apologize to Novus. They were all too proud. Too stubborn. Maybe Kire would have, were he not so angry that the love of his life had been kidnapped by her.

Kidnapped.

Thinking the simple words stirred something inside Kaos's head. He looked at Kire, still tied up in the ropes, still struggling to get out. Then he turned to Amberly, the smoke clearing more and more as their fight to get Rose back ensued. "Amberly, can you use your gauntlet to get those ropes off Kire?"

"I almost think he's safer like that," Trace muttered.

"Shut up!" Kire snapped.

"I can," Amberly said to Kaos.

"Good. Wrap her up with them."

Nodding, she held out a gauntlet-clad hand, her arm fully extended in front of her, and the ropes around Kire began unwinding and sliding off him. Above them, Novus fluttered overhead, trying to make an escape through the door.

"I don't think so!" Amberly shouted at her, aiming the ropes right at the fairy, manipulating them to snare her. Novus screamed and writhed in a panic. An angry, ferocious, desperate panic. But with her hands tied and her wings bound, she dropped to the ground with a painful thud, crying out.

She began sobbing, her sadness overtaking her anger. "It's all your fault! I just want her back!"

They stood in a circle around her, Kire dusting himself off. They were all braced and ready in case Novus made any sudden moves. They had her surrounded. They wouldn't let her get anywhere.

"Trace!" Novus cried. "How could you let them do this to me? How could *you* do this to me? After everything I did for you?"

"Where is Rose?" Kire asked.

Novus ignored him, taunting Trace instead. "Nobody wanted you, Trace. Nobody cared about you. Not even your own mother! I sat around listening to your pathetic sob stories despite my mother being dead because of you! And this is how you repay me? I was the only one who showed you any care. Who gave you any kindness!"

"He doesn't owe you anything," Amberly told her. "You're a liar. A snake. And you're wrong about Trace."

"Says the girl who broke his heart and tossed him aside like he was nothing!"

"For your information, not a day has gone by where I haven't loved Trace with everything I have. Maybe he thought nobody cared about him. Maybe *you* think you've been someone heroic and special, but you've done nothing. You *are* nothing. Now, either tell us where Rose is, or we'll kill you. Well, let Kire do it."

Novus's expression shifted to Kire, who had his fists balled, his facial expression resolved. He still hadn't changed his mind from earlier. He would kill Novus if he had to.

"I know what it's like to be manipulated," Trace said to her. "I should've seen this coming from you. But rest assured, Novus, if you've taught me anything, it's to not make this mistake ever again. You won't get any help from me."

They waited while Novus gritted her teeth, seeming to think it over. Then, finally, even though it was clear how desperately she didn't want to help them, she sagged under the ties of the magical rope. "Just take your stupid friend and never speak to me again."

"Where is she?" Kire said once again.

"She's in my shed out in the back garden."

"You guys stay here!" Kire shouted, the words flying quickly out of his mouth in a rush of eagerness. "In case she tries to pull anything else!" He darted out of the house.

"I'll go with him," Kaos called, knowing that, out of all of them, Amberly and Trace would be the best ones to keep Novus detained. He raced out of the cottage after Kire toward a small shack that looked a hundred years old, covered in moss and rotting wood planks. Kire's backpack shook awkwardly as he sprinted toward it, bursting inside and yelling, "Rose!"

By the time Kaos reached the doorway, a very filthy Rose covered in a smattering of cuts and bruises had been enveloped by Kire's arms.

"I thought the shed was so ancient and breakable that it would be easy to break out of." Rose was crying into Kire's neck. "But she must have enchanted it somehow. I couldn't escape, no matter what I tried. That's why I have all these bruises and cuts! I tried everything to get back to you guys. I swear I did!"

"It's going to be okay, Rose, it's going to be okay." Even though his back was to Kaos, Kaos could tell Kire was crying as well.

"Thank you," Rose said, her eyes meeting Kaos's gaze. "All of you."

"Well, that's one thing out of the way," Kaos said, leaning against the surprisingly sturdy door frame, wanting to diffuse the awkwardness of him interrupting their intimate moment. "Now, what do we do with the fairy?"

The solution ended up being rather simple and fair. Novus wouldn't have agreed, but the Defenders all did. None of them had it in them to kill somebody who wasn't directly trying to kill *them*. But Novus couldn't be trusted. They couldn't simply leave her alone and hope to never have a run-in with her again. She had no family. She'd hardly be missed in her community. She was dangerous, so their decision was to lock her in the prison they originally bought to hold Resin in. The small, magical contraption that kept her caged in between dimensions, where she could no longer harm anyone.

As they walked out of Novus's cottage, Kire's arm wrapped comfortingly over Rose's shoulders, the others smiling fondly at her, glad that she was safe. Amberly gave the device Novus was trapped inside of a hard shake. "Do you think this is doing anything to her in there?" she asked hopefully.

Kaos rolled his eyes.

"So... Amberly..." Trace called to her in a cocky voice. He wiggled his eyebrows as she stared at him. "Who knew you were such a romantic?"

Kaos knew he was referring to how she had sweetly defended Trace back inside Novus's cottage when she made the comment about loving Trace.

"I..." Looking uncomfortable, Amberly trailed off. Before

anyone else could say anything, Kire stopped walking, causing the others to slam into his back.

He slowly turned around to face them, his eyes widening.

"What is it?" Rose asked.

"What's that noise?" Amberly scrunched up her nose and tilted her head like a dog, hearing the squeak of a rubber toy.

Kaos stuck an ear out, and he heard it as well. A sort of vibration noise. It sounded like it was coming from Kire.

"It..." Kire's voice was shaky. "It's my backpack. I think it's Halo."

Now, Kaos understood Kire's weird expression. He realized what this meant. If Halo was waking up inside Kire's backpack, it could only mean one thing.

Halo was about to give the warning.

17

Having just heard Halo's warning, read aloud by Kire, the others stood around the open book, looking over his shoulder even though none of them could see anything Halo wrote except for Kire. To everyone else, the page remained blank as usual.

Kaos was reeling. Never had it seemed so real. Never before had the end of the world seemed so imminent. Just as they had guessed, Halo had awoken to give them the official warning. Yash's great attack was coming, and it was coming soon.

"We should get back home," Rose whispered softly. Kaos hardly even heard her because the words Kire had recited from Halo were still echoing loudly in his mind.

The time is now, young fighters. I have done the best I can to reserve any and all power I possess to keep an eye on the future and the ever-changing decisions of the great and powerful entity that is Yash. He intends to turn everything on the earth's surface to ash. And he's determined to not let anything stand in his way. If there was ever a time to get yourself prepared and ready, now would be that time.

"My parents," Rose continued with a sigh. "They have no idea where I am. Did you guys talk to them at all? Did they... Did they seem worried?"

Everyone's eyes went to Kire. He looked pale, as if there were other things on his mind than the memory of how he had shouted at Rose's parents.

"We can't go back," Trace said.

Amberly frowned. "We're not seriously starting this again, are we?"

"It's not that," he snapped. "We have our army. The people who want to help us. The people who can bring us to our world. We need to go speak to them. We need to go now."

"Are we really going to risk the lives of these villagers just to save our own world?" Rose asked.

"Rose," Kire said gently. "They want to fight."

"We're not forcing anyone to do anything," Kaos said. "Kire is right. They want to help. We should go talk to them."

"Maybe we should split up?" Trace said. "Some of us go back to our realm to make sure the destruction hasn't already begun. The rest of us go and talk to the army."

"We're not splitting up," Amberly demurred. "Not a chance. We're better together. Remember? That's kind of our whole... thing."

"Okay," Trace said with a huff, rolling his eyes, "then let's just be quick about it, shall we?"

All of Kaos's senses heightened because of the warning. He felt on edge, tense. He had a feeling in the back of his mind as he thought about the upcoming battle. Anxiety, possibly. It wasn't an emotion he was too familiar with.

Oof, these guys are rubbing off on me.

They hurried with the teleportation stone back to Albus, whom they knew would do a better job assembling the troops with his magical abilities than they all could. Albus worked fast, and within the hour, The Unlikely Defenders stood on a platform in front of a group of about a hundred people, all of whom looked up at them with determination, eager to listen.

"As much as I've enjoyed my time with you these past few days," Trace began. It was decided that he would speak since he had spent the most time with them all, training them and getting them ready to help. "The time has officially come for us to guide you back into the portal. To our realm. Mighty and powerful Yash, as foul as he is, is going to try and destroy our realm as he once tried to destroy yours."

"We're so grateful for your help. For your willingness to put your lives on the line to protect something that's not even yours," Rose added. It wasn't planned for her to say that, but Kaos decided it was a nice touch. Rose was a valuable addition to their group. He was seeing that more than ever.

The crowd of villagers cheered and raised their weapons in the air. They were ready for the fight.

But were the Defenders ready?

As the villagers cheered on the teens, Amberly tugged at Trace's sleeve, and he turned around. The quintets assembled in a huddle.

"What exactly did you train them to do?" she asked in a low voice. "Do you have a strategy or a plan?"

"What is it with you and your plans?" Kaos joked.

"It's always good to have a plan. It leaves little room for mistakes," she replied.

"But you can't predict the way things will turn out," Kire said. "Things don't always go according to plan."

"So?" Amberly said, ignoring her brother. "Trace, what did you teach them?"

"I don't know," Trace said with a shrug. "I sort of just explained that they need to fight with everything they've got and try to stay out of our way so that we can do the tough part and only intervene if they see us in great danger."

"Works for me," Kaos tried. Amberly shot him a glare.

"It's sort of hard to prepare for something we know nothing

about," Rose said to Amberly. "We don't know what we're fighting against. Yash is an entity. He is basically a god. Sure, we have magical abilities, but we're not *gods*. And we have no idea what awaits us inside that sinkhole. We have no idea what the battlegrounds are going to look like. We don't know what to expect, so how can we plan properly? I think Trace was right. They just have to fight. We all just have to fight and hope for the best outcome. We have to fight with everything we have."

"Who are you, and what did you do with my girlfriend?" Kire whispered in amazement as he beamed at Rose. She smiled at him sheepishly.

"I just…" Amberly's anger morphed into something unlike her. She seemed sad. Her shoulders sagged. "I don't know if I'll be able to take it if something happens to one of us. Any of us."

"We'll look out for each other," Kaos said, placing a hand on her shoulder. "We have this far, haven't we?"

"I guess."

"Oswald!" Trace called loudly, turning back to the crowd. A man Kaos recognized parted through the crowd. By looking at his commanding presence, the stern expression in his eyes, and his hard-set jaw, Kaos could tell he was someone in charge. Someone the others looked to. "You've trained your troops before for other battles in the past, correct?" Trace asked the man.

"Correct," Oswald replied. It occurred to Kaos why he looked familiar. He had been the one who led the villagers to Novus's cottage when they first expressed that they wanted to help the Defenders.

"Change of plans. I need you to stay here and continue that preparation. Get your weapons ready. Gather some strategies. Keep in mind that all of those magical beasts we destroyed here in your realm not long ago are going to be nothing compared to how powerful and strong Yash will be. Think you can handle it?"

"I'll do my best."

"Good. We're going to go back and scope out our realm. Once

we gather the intel, we'll come back and bring you over to the other side."

"Yes, sir." He raised a fist proudly in the air, a sign of unification, and the others followed, letting out a resounding collective grunt of confirmation.

Trace turned back around to the others. "That better?" he asked, looking mainly at Amberly.

"Actually, yes." She looked a little less tense than she had before. "You really have a way of addressing an entire group of people."

"I... do?"

Kaos watched the two of them stare at each other with googly eyes. And when they reached for each other's hands, they did it right in front of Kaos. It was as though they knew they could. They knew before Kaos himself had even been really sure that he would be okay with it. But Kaos was okay with it. It was inevitable for Trace and Amberly to rekindle their romance. They were meant to be together. Kaos had lied to himself about it for a long time, but deep down, he was sure he always knew. And they made sense together. More sense than Amberly made with him. Amberly and Kaos were both stubborn. Both full of fire. Both in need of control. They would butt heads. But Trace was the yin to her yang. They were the perfect balance for each other.

And Kaos was truly happy for them.

"Well, okay then," Kaos announced to his team, rubbing his hands together. "Let's get back home and, as Trace put it, 'gather some strategies'." He smirked at Trace, who playfully rolled his eyes, and it felt in that single moment like all was right in the world.

If only that were true.

18

When the Defenders returned to their realm once again, they retreated from the cave together. None of them spoke much as they took in their surroundings and saw that all was quiet. Yash had yet to begin further destruction. At least, not in Montgomery.

As they began their walk through The White Forest, they stayed silent. What really was there to say at this point? Would talking about the looming battle make it any easier to deal with once it came? Kaos didn't think so. He was fine in the quiet like this. It was nice to have a moment of respite, a moment of certainty. It was one thing to know that the most intense and dangerous battle was about to transpire, but it was almost nice to have a break from worrying about when they'd get the warning from Halo all the time.

"I'm sort of nervous," Rose admitted, being the first one to break the silence as they walked through the dense greenery surrounding them.

"To see your parents again?" Kire asked.

"Speaking of that," Amberly interjected, briefly pausing in her step. "What are we going to say? We can't explain that Rose was kidnapped without the police wanting to do a full investigation."

"We'll just say she got lost in the woods," Kaos said, thinking quickly. "It seems fitting, seeing as she's spent so much time in here anyway."

"Fair enough," Rose agreed.

"Okay..." Amberly put a contemplative finger to her chin. "Then we need to make it *look* like you've been missing in the woods."

"Do I not already?" Rose asked, examining her own body. "I feel completely disgusting."

"I'm so sorry, Rose," Kire said with gloomy eyes, keeping them downcast. "I should have been there. I should have never let this happen to you in the first place."

"If anyone should be apologizing, I think it's me," Trace argued ruefully. "I'm the one who trusted her, who made her my friend." Beside him, Amberly snorted. Trace let it slide.

"It's nobody's fault except for Novus's," Rose tried.

"Well, that and the fact that we are the reason her mom died," Kaos mumbled, knowing fully well it was probably an inappropriate comment to make at the time.

Everyone shot him dirty looks.

"*Anyway*," Rose continued with a headshake. "She didn't even hurt me. She just kept me locked up in that shed. She tricked me by saying that we owed her a favor from when she lent us the money to get the materials to capture Rezin. And that you can't break a promise to a fairy."

"What favor did she want anyway?" Trace asked.

"She wanted to know about Yash. About when the battle was going to be. She actually wanted to be on *his* side, believe it or not. I was not any help, though, because I didn't have much info to give her. She hated that."

"Well, she's one heck of an actress," Trace said bitterly. "I had no idea she hated us so much."

"I did," Amberly said.

"Amberly," Kire barked. "We get it. You didn't like her. We all know it's not because she gave off bad vibes—it's because you were jealous."

At that, Amberly shut her mouth. The comment only made Trace smile at her. As much as she tried not to, she couldn't help but smile back. Then she turned her attention back to Rose. "You need more dirt."

For the next few minutes, the group took turns sticking various twigs in Rose's hair, smattering her with semi-dry mud, and making her clothes look as though they'd been torn and sodded while she ran through bushes and low-hanging branches.

"All right, I think that's good," Amberly said afterward. "I hope you're ready, because you are the talk of the town."

"*Lovely*, we all know how much I *love* being the center of attention," Rose said dryly.

"Well, with Halo's warning, you won't be the center of attention for long," Trace pointed out. Rose swallowed audibly.

The group had to be crafty as they exited The White Forest. Rose expressed she had no desire to interact with law enforcement and the rescue team that had their vehicles parked outside the entrance to the hiking trails. She just wanted to go back to her family and deal with that first.

Sneaking around Montgomery as they made their way back to Rose's residence, all was quiet still. No one seemed in a panic. No one was running out of their house, yelling about how the world was ending. That meant they had time, time for Rose to reunite with her family. While it hadn't been a long time since she had been gone in Montgomery, she had been separated from everybody for a while in the Albus realm.

Eventually, they reached the exterior of Rose's house. The light on the porch was on, and the sun outside was setting. Kaos expected it to be busier, but he supposed everyone was out searching and not waiting around Rose's house in hopes of her showing up out of the blue like this.

"Do you want me to go with you?" Kire whispered, catching the uneasy expression on Rose's face as she stared at her front door.

"I..." She took her sweet time deciding on the answer when the front door suddenly opened. A very tired Beverly Rose squinted out at them.

"Who's here?" she asked. "What do you want?" She was probably exhausted and sick of all the people requesting news stories and police asking questions. But upon realizing it was her daughter's face among the teenagers standing out on the street, her expression changed in a split second. Her eyes widened. She inhaled a gasp. Her hand went to her mouth. "Charlie?" she whispered, as if she was afraid to be wrong. Then she got louder. "Charlie! It's you!" She ran down the porch steps to throw her arms around Rose. Upon hearing his wife scream, Tim Rose also appeared in the doorway. When he saw what was happening, he sprinted across the lawn to join them in their family hug. Kaos and the others stepped away, letting them have their moment. Rose was slightly stiff in her parents' arms, but she hugged them back, nonetheless. They both cried into her hair and breathed sighs of relief.

"I thought I lost you forever! What happened?" her mom asked.

"Are you hurt?" Tim asked. "Should I get an ambulance over here?"

"No, don't!" Rose squeaked out. "I'm okay, really. I was just... lost."

"Lost?" Her mother repeated, her eyebrows bustling together.

"Okay. As long as you're not hurt, the rest can wait," Tim said, squeezing Rose tighter to him. "All that matters is that you're back safe."

"I... " Rose gently stepped away from them. "I didn't think you'd care so much."

With that, both her parents' eyes went immediately to Kire. Noticing it, Rose checked over her shoulder at him. The expression of confusion on Rose's face was clear. When she turned back to her parents, their eyes were back on her.

"We know we haven't been the best parents to you, Rose. And we're so sorry for that. But I promise you. Things are going to change. I don't ever want to think I lost you again," her mom said.

"I can't tell you how sorry I am that we ever made you feel as though we didn't love you. We do," her dad said. "And we're going to do a better job showing it."

Seeing the disbelief in Rose's eyes was classic. It even stirred up emotion in the usually numb Kaos. He thought of his own parents, of how they would react if he had gone missing. He knew they'd be sad. It did often annoy him how busy they were with work and how they were often too invested in their son's life, but it came from a good place. They just wanted the best for him. Kaos could appreciate that.

As he watched Rose and her parents embrace in another sweet reuniting hug, Kaos wanted to keep his family safe more than ever. Whatever it took.

19

I t amazed Kaos how, in the blink of an eye, everything could suddenly change. As he, Trace, Amberly, and Kire stood outside Rose's house, watching the sweet reunion and the promises her parents made for a better future for their daughter, the ground suddenly began to rumble. Rose and her parents were so lost in their own little world for a moment that they didn't realize what the other four did. Something was happening. And it didn't look good.

"Is that...?" Amberly began.

"An earthquake?" Trace finished for her.

The rumbling grew louder. The pavement shook under their feet. Finally, Rose and her parents looked up, sensing the danger.

"This can't be happening right now," Amberly whispered, terror washing over her.

But it was. It was Yash. It had to be.

"All of you," Rose's dad called urgently. "Inside the house. Now."

But none of them moved. As Tim tried to push Rose in the direction of the front door, she resisted.

"It's not safe out here, come on!" he cried.

"Rose, what are you doing?!" her mom squeaked.

The teens couldn't go into Rose's house. They couldn't even go back to the Albus realm to grab their army.

"Halo didn't tell us it would happen *this* quickly!" Kire cried out.

"What are you talking about?" Rose's dad asked. "Please just come inside, will you?"

"I can't, Dad," Rose said. She put a hand on his forearm and looked at him with determined eyes. "We have to go."

"Go where?"

Rose looked at the others, and Kaos nodded at her. They had to go to the sinkhole. The rumbling was getting worse. People were pulling their cars over and jumping out, looking for somewhere to hide. The sky above them darkened. Heavy, thick clouds seemed to appear out of nowhere.

"We're going to fix this," Rose told her parents. She left their side to join the Defenders. "I promise," she called to them.

"Rose, stop it right now," her mom pleaded.

The roaring of the earthquake that Yash was undoubtedly causing was now so loud that they could no longer hear each other speaking. The facades of houses began to crumble. Glass shattered in windowpanes. People screamed in the distance.

"We've got to move," Kaos instructed. He was more nervous now than ever. He had anticipated having help. On going into that sinkhole with more than just the five of them.

"I'm sorry," Rose called to her parents. Then she nodded at the others, and they took off running toward the sinkhole.

"What are we going to do?" Amberly asked in a panic. "What about our army?"

"Well, we never had one before," Trace said. "We didn't need it then; we don't need it now. We've defeated all of the other alien scum Yash sent down. We've done what no one else has been able to. So we can do this, too."

Kaos would have loved to believe him. He was prepared to give this battle everything he had, but he was confident that it would not be enough. Not without their army.

Still, they approached the sinkhole. Down in its depths, it emitted an otherworldly glow. It was like an invitation, calling to the Defenders, telling them it was time. Without further ado, they climbed over the edge of the sinkhole, the mud so slick despite the chunks of broken-up asphalt and crumbling buildings that they slid right to the deepest center of it. Like stuck in quicksand, Kaos yelled his instructions to the others to hold their breath, and then he closed his eyes, inhaled deeply, and readied himself. Before he knew it, he was pulled under by an unknown force.

He was overcome with the sensation of floating through space and time, similar to how it felt to go through the portal between the Albus realm and their realm. His feet lifted off the ground. A powerful wind rushed through his hair. Everything spun around him. And then, out of nowhere, he was back on his feet.

In pitch-black nothingness.

"Guys?" he called.

"We're here," Amberly said, her voice close to Kaos even though he couldn't see her. He couldn't see anything.

He stood very still. How were they supposed to fight Yash if they couldn't even see him? Was that the whole point?

Just then, the ground underneath someone's feet glowed as they took a step forward. It was as if they were stepping into a puddle of neon light. It glowed a brilliant hot pink.

"Whoa," Rose said. She took a step. It glowed neon orange. The more they walked around, the more they moved as a group, the easier it was to see better. Then, Kaos noticed Trace pull out his sword and light it on fire. The glow helped. They could see each other, sure. But five feet in front of where the fire stopped illuminating? Still nothing. Nothing around them in any direction.

"Do you think this is Yash's ship?" Kire asked.

"Do you think he's here?" Amberly added. It sent a shudder down Kaos's spine. Was there Yash? What could they expect from him? How was this going to go? He hated the unknown. He tried to use the magic on his crown to search for thoughts, to find a body he could command. But nothing came.

Go figure.

A cool breeze rushed over him, but then it disappeared just as quickly. It was like a ghost had just floated right past his head.

"Did you guys feel that?" he asked.

"What was that?" Rose whispered.

"Everyone, just be ready," Kaos instructed. He swallowed audibly. "Try to stay together as much as possible. Kire, do you think Halo's going to be able to help us out at all?"

"I guess we'll see."

If Halo couldn't protect Kire, then they had to work twice as hard to make sure they could help him. Halo was Kire's only weapon.

They waited. They walked, illuminating the ground in different neon colors with each step as Trace's sword lit their way. Every so often, the cold breeze would come back and go away again. Where they were going, they didn't know. How they would get out of here, they also didn't know.

They all stopped moving when, a few feet ahead of them, the tiniest flash of a bright green neon light appeared on the ground as though a raindrop had fallen. But that one single drop, instead of darkening and disappearing, began to spread and ripple outward in a massive circle. Growing larger and larger. Its colors changed like the Defenders were at some sort of dance party. But it was silent. Silent in a way that had Kaos feeling deeply unsettled. The neon ripple expanded even under their feet. It spread out all around them, maybe for miles. It moved fast, silent, and viscous. It would've been mesmerizing if they weren't in such danger.

The cold breeze came back, but this time, it stayed. It drenched Kaos, and he straightened his crown on his head, making sure it was extra secure.

Then, quicker than Kaos could even blink, it was dark again except for the light from Trace's sword.

Still, the chill was there.

"I..." Rose whispered. "I sensed something."

"What do you mean?" Trace asked. He aimed his sword in her direction to illuminate her features. Silently, Rose lifted a hand and pointed at something behind all of them. They turned, and right at the same spot where the raindrop-like color of neon appeared, two glowing red slits now illuminated in the dark.

Eyes.

"Guys," Kire said uneasily. "I think that's—"

He was cut off when a burst of wind so powerful knocked them all off their feet and threw them backward. Sinister laughter rang out, loud enough to be heard across an entire football stadium.

It was Yash.

20

Quickly, they all scrambled to their feet as neon-illuminated footsteps grew nearer to them in the distance. When Yash was close enough to be lit by Trace's fiery sword, the Defenders were face-to-face with their worst enemy: the entity who threatened to destroy everything they ever knew. And *they* were the ones who had to stop him.

"Now," Yash's amplified voice began, his mouth moving with a slight lag compared to the rate at which he spoke, as if it took his voice a long time to travel from him to the speaker surrounding them. "I'd stand here and start off by commending you for getting this far."

He was so strange-looking. He was naturally tall, well over seven feet. But he was slender, his body moving with a snake-like quality whenever he spoke or took another step toward them. Aside from the glowing red slits for eyes, his height, and his too-skinny build, his other features were relatively normal. He didn't even look that old, though he surely was. But Kaos supposed that was another power Yash possessed; he could appear however he wanted to. And he apparently preferred to look like a normal human who had been stretched like taffy.

"Your kind is so pathetic," he went on. "Even at this moment, you probably carry hope inside of you. Hope that you'll somehow be strong enough to make it through this. It disgusts me. Hope is weak. There's no room for it in my world. In any world. Which is why yours must be destroyed. And I'm done wasting time."

Everything happened so fast. There was wind, calm and powerful enough to lift them all into the air again. Rain splashed down, the droplets illuminating everything around them, the bright neon reflecting off it with an almost blinding effect. Someone screamed, but Kaos couldn't see the other quintets. It sounded like Amberly. And it sounded like Amberly had somehow gotten far away from him.

There was shouting—Trace's angry rage. Balls of fire soared through the air, a fiery sword slashing around.

A great wall of blue fire appeared from nothing; a tsunami headed right for them. Kaos was going to be burned before he even had time to make a single move against his opponent. How pathetic could he be? How could any of them have ever seriously thought they could defeat Yash?

The wave of fire loomed over their heads, and just as it was about to swallow them up, an invisible barrier held it back.

Halo's shield.

Acting fast, Amberly manipulated the rain to create a larger wall of water to spill over the fire, extinguishing it. Then beside her, Trace began screaming in complete agony at the top of his lungs, as though he were being physically tortured by something or someone.

"I'm on fire!" he shouted at the others. "I'm on fire! HELP ME!"

But he wasn't on fire. This had to be the doing of Yash, only making Trace *feel* like he was.

"Amberly!" Kaos roared.

As if reading his mind, Amberly brought the wall of water over Trace, drenching him with it.

"Trace?" Amberly squeaked in the darkness. Trace's yelling had ceased.

"Shut up, Amberly, no one loves you," his voice said, sounding so sinister and unlike himself that it sent literal chills down Kaos's spine.

"W-what?" Amberly asked.

"It's true," Yash's booming voice replied. "I've been to the other side. I've spoken with your mother, Amberly McHenry. She was happy to die. Happy to be free of you."

"Don't listen to him!" Kaos shouted.

"Yash—he made me say it, Amberly!" Trace called out in a panic.

Yash was nowhere and everywhere all at once. He changed the laws of every reality they ever knew. He could create anything he wanted here. He could make anything happen with a single thought.

"Keep going, guys! Come on!" Kaos urged. He wasn't hopeful. He was desperate. He wondered if Yash knew the difference.

Suddenly, Kaos couldn't breathe. He tried, but it felt like he sucked in a mouthful of water. Suddenly, he was weightless, floating. It was like he was underwater, but he was dry. Gravity was gone, at least for him. Even though he was panicking, he kept one hand on his crown to prevent it from slipping off and floating away. Somewhere he couldn't see, another one of the quintets cried out as though they were in agonizing pain. Kaos was too far away again to know what was happening.

In the distance, Rose shouted, "Stop it! No! It's not true!"

As Kaos flailed about in zero gravity, drowning on a mouthful of invisible water, he wondered what Yash was doing to Rose. If he was making her see things that weren't true. How could he attack all of them at once like this? They couldn't even see where he was. He could be nowhere. He could be everywhere. He could be on all of them at the same time.

And at any point now, Kaos's lungs would burst. He would die, leaving the others to fight without him.

Though it was hard to concentrate on anything but the drowning and his friends all in danger around him, he tried the best he could to use his crown to get Yash to stop. It didn't take long for him to realize it was useless. For his mind began to fade. For his frantic struggling to slow.

Just as he thought this was the end for him, he slammed into the ground, his arm breaking with a loud crack as he landed on it. He yelled out in pain, but he was, in truth, relieved to be feeling it. Because that meant he was still alive. It meant he could still fight.

It was black all around them again. There wasn't even a cold chill this time. There were no neon glows apart from wherever they touched the ground.

"What just happened?" Amberly's voice asked in the darkness. She sounded out of breath.

"Halo," Kire said, scrambling in the light of Trace's flames to get to his book, which was glowing as it lay open on the ground. Halo must've put a shield around all of them, a shield impenetrable even to Yash. This shield was different. It was stronger. It created a dome around them large enough for them all to move about. It was soundproof. A pitch-black veil that hid them out of sight from anything that was happening on the outside of it. Kaos had never seen Halo produce anything like it.

"Is there a message?" Kaos asked Kire, clutching his arm and hurrying after him.

"Halo wants us to get out of here," Kire informed them as he read the book's latest note that no one else could see. "A compass!" Kaos squinted down at the page of the book. Sure enough, Halo had drawn a moving, working compass. This one was unique. Instead of the typical NESW labels, it had only one. Montgomery in small, swirly lettering.

"Leave? Now?" Trace asked.

"Just to retreat and regroup," Kire explained. "Halo knows we can't take Yash on our own! Not like this!" Kire started walking with Halo in both of his hands, and the others kept close behind him to stay in the protection of the shield. "The shield over us, it's doing something to Yash. To us. Keeping us hidden from him. For the time being."

"Even a stupid book knows we can't do this," Amberly said. The book started to shake, harder and harder the closer they reached, wherever it was in the pitch-black darkness Halo was guiding them toward. Then, in a single instant, the five teens soared through time and space once more, landing suddenly back in Montgomery, back outside the sinkhole.

"Oh my God," Rose uttered, but it took Kaos a second to look up and see why because he was too busy nursing his broken arm. It was healing quickly, which he was thankful for. Faster than he had ever healed before.

Montgomery was in bad shape. All around them, buildings had collapsed entirely. They lay in crumbled heaps, the streets buried under smoke and dust. Every car alarm was going off at once. All of the windshield wipers were behaving erratically. Every car window that hadn't been shattered rolled up and down, up and down. People screamed. Dogs barked. Most people ran. Some of them couldn't get up.

"What are we going to do?" Trace asked. "Yash is going to destroy everything! What do we *do*?!"

Everyone around them was in such a panic that no one noticed how they had all just poofed out of nowhere in front of the sinkhole. Kaos turned back to it, staring down. Somehow, from inside that sinkhole, Yash was able to control things happening out here.

He straightened his crown.

Who's to say I can't reach Yash's mind on the other side from here? Kaos wondered. Maybe with Yash being on his ship, he wouldn't be able to stop Kaos from reading his mind. Kaos tried to picture an exact location of where Yash was, beyond the sinkhole, longing for his powers to allow him to search for the monster and his thoughts.

"Kaos, what are you doing?" Amberly asked in a panic. "Get back over here."

Kaos continued searching, thinking harder than he ever had about anything. He held his focus, letting nothing else distract him. It was him and this moment, him and this one chance to see inside Yash, to figure out his plan.

Finally, his powers connected, and he felt himself become an overcharged circuit. It started at his head and spread through his body, down his arms and legs, and out his fingers and toes. He felt excruciating pain, like something had him chained to an electrified fence. He yelled out and dropped to his knees, but he would not break this connection no matter how much pain it caused him. He needed to see the way to stop Yash. He needed to gain control.

He heard yelling. A loud, booming yell. Yash crying out with fury. Pain, even. Pain Kaos caused by being in his head. But it was brief, cut off as if somebody hit the power button on a TV remote.

When Kaos returned to the present, his entire body shook, and he was on his back on the ground, the chaos of the world around him at a standstill.

"What just happened?" Trace asked at his side, Amberly close behind him.

Kaos was exhausted. In pain. He had no idea how to answer. And he didn't know why he felt so sure when he replied with, "I... I weakened him. I connected with him and... And... I focused hard on commanding him to stop his existence. I don't think it worked. But maybe he harmed himself. I don't know. I lost the connection."

"Are you okay?" Amberly asked.

"I'll be fine."

Already, Kaos's arm was nearly back to normal. He was still healing faster than he ever had before. Was that because of the others? Because of their united front? Maybe they were stronger together than they had ever been, but they hadn't even had a chance to show off what they could do back on Yash's ship. Yash had been simply too much.

"So... you weakened him. But not entirely. He's not entirely... You know, finished?" Trace clarified. Kaos shook his head.

"Not even close."

There was no telling how much time they had. There was no way of knowing when Yash would be strong enough to continue his attack. When the world would be in complete chaos once again. The group had to be quick with their decision-making. The result was that they split up, even though they knew it was risky. Kaos and Kire were to rush back to the Albus realm to grab their army and return to the sinkhole as soon as possible. Their strongest fighters—Trace with his sword, Amberly with her gauntlet, and Rose with her plant and animal manipulating powers—were to stay in case they needed to keep fighting and holding Yash off until the others returned.

"Well," Kire said to Kaos as they looked at the options of abandoned cars littering the streets of their town, "Which one should we take?"

"That's funny coming from you. And this is going to sound funny coming from me," Kaos told him, "but we don't exactly have the luxury of being picky right now. Come on, let's go!"

When the gang had come up with this splitting-up idea while they were discussing their options, Kire had written into Halo, asking if there could be a way for it to notify them if they were needed back in the Earth realm before they got their army, in case of an emergency. Halo had complied, saying that it was possible. So, the book didn't go back in Kire's backpack as he and Kaos selected a plain-looking SUV, Kaos hopping into the driver's seat while Kire climbed into the passenger. Halo stayed open in Kire's hands; he wanted to see the book's alert as soon as it appeared in case they needed to get back.

With police everywhere, buildings on fire, debris from crumbled buildings, and cars parked and abandoned in the middle of the street around every corner Kaos turned, he had to get a little crazy with his driving, going up on sidewalks and swerving into the wrong lane. At one point, a police officer tried to flag him down, but the officer was on foot, and Kaos easily left him in the dust.

"Hang on tight," Kaos told Kire as they approached The White Forest. "Things are about to get bumpy."

He had no experience off-roading, and as the SUV hopped the curb and drove into the trees, he had a difficult time keeping control of the steering wheel while bouncing around in his seat over bumps and jolts and sharp turns.

"What exactly are we going to do if we get the army back over here?" Kire said, his voice shaking due to the rumbling of the vehicle on the rocky terrain. "It's not like we can fit a hundred people in this SUV!"

"No problem," Kaos said. "We'll just run back."

"And what if we run into the police officer again? Or another one? What are they going to think when they see a massive crowd of people dressed like they're going to Comi-Con to see the Zelda exhibit?"

"Kire, there's going to be a hundred of us. A hundred of us going to fight Yash. I think we can handle an officer on our way there. Montgomery's got enough problems without worrying about people roaming the streets."

"You're probably right. Sorry. I'm just nervous. I need this to work."

"*We* need to make this work," Kaos corrected. "Hive mindset, right?"

"Right."

Soon enough, the trees got too dense, too close together for Kaos to continue driving by car. They got out and went on foot the rest of the way, running, Kire continually falling behind because he had to juggle the backpack on his shoulders as well as the opened ancient book in his hands.

The boys got to the Albus realm. They teleported to Oswald's training ground, where their troop was hard at work. From there, everything happened quickly. They found Oswald, explained the situation, and Oswald had everyone rallied and ready to go in minutes. It was easy to forget that they could take their time here. That only a couple of seconds would have gone by by the time they returned to their realm. Kaos still sensed the strong urgency; they needed to get their army over to their realm as quickly as they could.

The various men and women volunteer fighters followed behind Oswald, who followed behind Kaos and Kire on their way to the portal, where all of these Albus realm dwellers would be experiencing the Earth realm for the first time. Kire and Kaos tried the best they could to explain over their shoulders what they could expect from Yash, what was happening in their world, and how they should be prepared.

"Halo hasn't said anything yet, right?" Kaos double-checked with Kire as they jogged along, like first-place leaders in a long, competitive race.

"Not yet."

"So things are still good on the other side?"

"I hope so."

They stopped once they reached the portal. Kaos turned and

faced everyone. "This is your last chance. Once we go to the other side, there may be no turning back. If you no longer wish to help, leave. Now."

He stared them all down. Nobody moved an inch. They all stared back at him with earnest, ready-to-fight eyes.

"All right then." He had a strange urge to yell out, 'This is Sparta!' but refrained. Instead, he swallowed nervously. He felt guilty, like he had to use his crown to make them all agree to fight for him. How could he possibly be worth it otherwise? How could the strangers be so willing to protect them? To lay their life on the line for them? How was it that Kaos didn't even have to use his crown?

He looked at Kire, who was again checking Halo for any messages. "You go through the portal and meet them on the other side, and I'll send them through one by one, and then I'll go through last."

Kire nodded. He shouldered the backpack and squeezed the book tightly to his chest; then, he disappeared through the arch, showing the others how it was done.

When the last member of their army was through the portal, Kaos braced himself. He hoped Yash was ready for them. Or better yet, he hoped they returned to the battle with so much help that they would catch Yash completely off guard.

Hope wasn't pitiful. Hope was power.

"WHAT SORT OF TREE IS THAT?"

"Is that some sort of carriage? Where are the horses?"

"Your world is in a lot worse shape than ours. Does it always look like this?"

"What is that smell? It's awful."

The Albus realm beings were overwhelmed with their questions about how Earth worked. As the large group watched together, Kaos checked another text message from his mom, asking where he was and if he was okay. Seeing the message gave him the split-second idea to change course while things were still calm, as Yash had not yet resumed his attack on Earth. Kaos called Trace, instructing him to meet back at his place with Rose and Amberly.

The two groups converged at the massive inclining driveway in front of Kaos's home.

"That is *some* cottage," someone remarked. Another whistled. Kaos greeted his friends and led them up the driveway, bringing everyone into his home through the open garage. Stepping inside, he braced himself for what he was about to do.

"Mom, Dad?" he called to his family.

"We're over here," they responded from the sofa.

Others started filing into the house after him, and when they reached them, Kaos's parents stood from where they had been cuddled up on the couch, their faces twisting in complete shock at the sight of all the strange people suddenly standing in their home —the men and women in their peculiar attire carrying dangerous weapons.

"What the..." Kaos's dad breathed, too stunned to finish his sentence.

"Kaos?" his mom said, her eyes flitting between her son and the newcomers. "What... What is going on here?"

"The earthquakes and fires, the reason why Montgomery is suddenly falling apart, I know why," Kaos began.

"Okay, but that isn't going to explain—"

Kaos cut his mom off. "It will explain why I have these people here with me. I promise."

His mother and father exchanged a glance.

Kaos continued. "Our world is under attack. And the reason I wear this crown is because it gives me a special gift. Trace, Amberly, Kire, and Rose? They've all got gifts too. Because we are the ones who have to save us all."

"Is it some sort of joke?" his dad snapped, his eyebrows narrowing.

"Because if it is," his mom added, "I don't understand it. Kaos, who are these people?"

"Just—" Kaos tried to press down his frustration. "Mom, watch Dad."

Using his abilities, Kaos focused on his father, using his mind control to make him pat his head and rub his belly at the same time —something obscene to see at a time like this, and also unlike his father because his whole life, it had been an ongoing joke how his father had never been able to do that maneuver.

"What's happening?" his mom stammered, staring at her husband in horror as if she just watched him murder a crowd of people instead of doing some simple hand gestures.

"I'm controlling him with my mind. I can control you, too. And I can read your thoughts. Right now, you're thinking that this is impossible, but at the same time, you believe me."

She grew even more shocked. Kaos stopped controlling his father, who cleared his throat and stood tall, trying not to look embarrassed.

"I... I'm not sure what just happened," he admitted.

"Dad, you're thinking that you're angry at me for making you look stupid in front of all these people."

"How did you...?"

"I don't have time to answer any questions," Kaos said. "Just trust me when I say that all of these people are from another realm, and they're going to help us fight the person that's causing this whole mess. This is one of the only spaces I could think of big enough to hold everyone. And it's also impervious to many types of natural disasters." His father had put a lot of time and money into fortifying their house so it would stand for years to come. "You have nothing to worry about; none of them are going to hurt you," Kaos continued. "But in order for us to be able to keep you safe, to keep the whole world safe, you have to allow them to be here. Just for a while."

He was getting through to his parents. He only used his control over them as an example, not as the only solution to get them to do what he wanted. He was having a real, open, honest conversation with them. He almost forgot what that felt like; he had been manipulating them for so long. And he just didn't want to be that guy anymore.

"What do we do?" his mom asked his dad. His dad stared at Kaos for a long while. Then, with the other members of their army standing behind him, having his back, Kaos thought his dad looked proud. Bewildered, yes. But also proud.

"I guess we let them stay," he told his wife with an incredulous shrug.

"Okay, to the loft then," Kaos instructed the others, swelling with pride. His father was seeing him be a leader. He wasn't sure there was another feeling that could top that.

"What's a loft?" someone called.

"We're going upstairs," Rose explained to them. Up there, Kaos had a massive hangout space. While it was still cramped, they fit almost comfortably—at least well enough to talk and plan while they waited for Yash to stop hiding and resume trying to destroy their realm.

"When we get back to his 'ship,' there's not going to be any wasting time. You might not be able to see Yash. You might not even be able to feel him. But he'll be there. You all need to be on your guard," Kaos instructed. It felt good to have everyone so receptive and so willing to agree to his ideas. It was one thing for the other members of the Defenders to willingly let him lead, but for a group of strangers to allow a teenager to do so as well was a powerful feeling.

They talked battle strategies among themselves for a brief while, but eventually, Halo shot out a warning, sensing that danger was near once more. She hadn't been good about giving them enough warning last time, so there was no time to waste now.

"I just want to thank you all for helping us," Kaos said. "We already tried to do this without you, and we weren't cut out for it. Now, we have a real chance at saving this world. And it's because of you."

This time, the Defenders quite possibly had a real shot.

22

Even as they made their way back to the sinkhole, one big group banded together, ready to stop the evil Yash, the destruction around them resumed. The ground rumbled with an earthquake in a way that felt unnatural to Kaos. He knew it wasn't nature doing this; it was Yash. He checked on his companions, looking over his shoulder, glad to see that they didn't look fazed by their dangerous surroundings. They weren't shaken; they were ready to keep going.

"Dad," a teenage boy said behind Kaos. When he looked over his shoulder at him, he found a kid putting a hand on Oswald's shoulder. "I know that this world may end and everything, but if it doesn't, can we check this place out for real? It's so different!"

Oswald chuckled, as though they were just going for a casual stroll in a world that wasn't falling apart around them.

"You know, Edward, I was thinking the exact same thing."

Edward, Oswald's son, fell back, and Kaos eyed the Albus realm's troop leader.

"I didn't know you had a son that was going to take part in the battle," Kaos said to him. He didn't feel right about it. Something felt off, wrong. They seemed like they had such a good family dynamic. The perfect father and son pair, and potentially getting themselves killed, was their way of spending quality time together?

"Oh, Edward's always trying to prove himself," Oswald said with a proud smile, very similar to the one Kaos's father had given him a short while ago. Kaos cleared his throat uncomfortably and nodded, turning away from the man.

The plan was simple enough, but as it had been mentioned earlier, things didn't always go according to plan. They just had to go in and hope for the best. They were all to go back into the sinkhole, band together in a large clump in the blackness of Yash's ship between realms, and start their attack outwards, firing in any random direction necessary as long as they didn't aim toward the middle. They stayed as one unit, sticking together. One hundred of them and only one of Yash.

They entered the sinkhole once more, landing in the nothingness for possibly the final time. Their landing created a glowing neon light beneath their feet. With one hundred of them, one hundred pairs of glowing, neon footsteps, it made seeing their surroundings a great deal easier.

Feeling strong and ready to fight, Kaos really did see the beauty in all of the mixed neon colors lighting up their corner of Yash's ship around them.

"You will remember what Kaos said!" Trace's voice boomed in the darkness to their army. "There's no time to waste! It doesn't matter if you can't see him! Aim and fire!"

And so, round two of the battle against Yash began.

There was little the great and powerful entity could do to remain hidden as medieval weapons went off all around him. Rose's vines, strong and thick, grew out of nothing, soaring through the air, searching for a throat to wrap their thorny strands around. The cold air came back. So did the waves of Yash's fire, the flames a brilliant blue, further lighting up their surroundings. The shouts of terror from Yash made people see things that weren't really there. Battle cries and wounded cries sounded from every direction. Kaos almost fell over in the wind as he looked around for a familiar face among the battlers. He and the Defenders needed to stick together; he needed them. They needed him. They were better together.

"It was foolish of you to bring all of these men and women to die!" Yash's voice reprimanded loudly through a sort of invisible speaker. "They'll all die for nothing! You will not win this fight!"

"We'll see about that!" Kire's voice rang out. Kaos smirked, thinking Kire had come a long way from the boy he was at the beginning of all of this. Kaos decided to take a page from Kire's book and channel his confidence; he wouldn't let these people die for nothing.

Focus, Kaos. He calmed his breathing, stopped letting his surroundings distract him, and kept his focus on one thing only. Yash. Kaos tried to sense him, to get a good read on him like he had when he was outside the portal. If he could just access him, one little tidbit of insight or one little attempt at manipulation could change everything.

It was even harder this time than before, with all these bodies in close proximity, all fighting together against the balls of magic, the fire of Yarra, and Yash's reality-bending manipulation tactics, generally having close to the same trains of thought—*Don't die*— making things difficult. Where was Yash?

The more Kaos tried, the more frustrated he got and the more intense things became. Maybe he wasn't trying as hard as he could because he was terrified of that feeling of being electrocuted happening a second time. He'd do almost anything to avoid feeling that kind of pain again. And maybe because of that, part of his brain was purposely keeping him from making contact again, focusing on everyone else, on the easier thoughts to handle, on the easier people to control—than the ones that wanted to electrocute him.

He needed to man up. Screams around him were beginning to sound less like battle cries and more like terrified cries. He knew people were in danger. He could sense that everyone in his group was still okay, though he didn't know how. It was just this feeling of uncertainty in the pit of his gut telling him they were hanging on just fine. While Kaos still felt strong, he was nervous, unsettled, and afraid of things going from bad to worse, to horrific, all because these naive teenagers were willing to let so many others risk their lives to help them.

A ball of light flew right in his direction, and he rolled out of the way, barely dodging it in time. Maybe it was unintentional. It didn't seem like one of Yash's usual moves, not that he really knew what that would look like. He pondered if there were other people now joining his army, other minions, ones powerful like Rezin, Heno, and Jago. It had been quite a feat in itself to have to end those three minions one at a time. But what if Yash had saved his most powerful minions for this? And they had to defeat multiple of them at once, on *top* of defeating Yash?

Despair lodged in his throat. He wanted to cry out that this wouldn't work, that they should give up, call it quits, and just plead with Yash instead. But deep down, he knew that wouldn't work either. Yash didn't want them to beg for mercy; he just wanted to see their world burn. Kaos had no choice but to keep moving and keep fighting.

"Kaos!" Trace's voice called right when he needed it most. "I don't know where Yash is. There's too much going on! He's every-where all at once! Try to track him with your mind!"

Kaos gritted his teeth and nodded, not even sure where Trace was amid all the chaos.

You can do this, he told himself, picturing his dad there, coaching him, even applying the pressure a little too thick like he liked to do.

"I can do this."

He took a deep breath and focused, tuning out the shouts, cries, and noises of sheer terror. He focused on his breathing, on the magic of his crown flowing through his body. With good concentration, he did a mind search, jumping from head-to-head, trying to reach the one he was most eager to find.

He's much too powerful, one voice thought. Not Yash's. A villager's.

Maybe this wasn't such a good idea, another villager's voice said.

The pain! The pain! I'll never get through it!

Also not Yash.

The next voice Kaos heard in his mind was full of complete mental anguish. Quickly, their thoughts drifted into oblivion.

That couldn't be Yash, either.

After a couple more of hearing thoughts like this, ones that faded out into nothing, Kaos finally figured it out—he was jumping into the minds of people who were dying.

"No, no, no, no, no!" he shouted, gripping his crown, wanting to hurl it away from him so he never had to hear anything like it again. People were dying!

What had he and the others been thinking? There was no way they could win!

Kaos almost couldn't control it now as he jumped to another mind.

Where is Esmeralda? She was just here. I need to make sure she's safe. I—

"Duck!" Kaos shouted at the man, who was too busy searching for his Esmeralda to realize a giant fireball was headed straight for him. Just in the nick of time, the man ducked, his life spared. With huge eyes, he turned to Kaos.

"Th-thank you," the man sputtered, astonished that he had nearly been turned to ash a single millisecond.

"Just hang in there," Kaos instructed. He used his mind control then. Not on Yash, but on this man. He manipulated him into being more alert, better at multitasking, a better fighter. All this time, Kaos had been playing offense, trying to focus his powers on his opponents. He hadn't considered the other option— focusing on his fighters, using his mind-controlling abilities to make them better at what they were doing, less afraid, more confident.

I don't want to do this anymore! he heard another voice crying. Using the tunnel vision that buzzed through his veins, he pinpointed exactly who said it—a woman who looked old enough to be his mother, her shoulders sagging in defeat, her face splattered with something red and dark. Kaos manipulated her next. *Act confident. Act as though you know exactly what you're doing, and you know exactly the right way to protect yourself and aid in this fight.*

She straightened up, rolled her bony shoulders back, and her eyes narrowed, the look of distress gone. With a war cry, she charged into the abyss of battle.

That worked! Kaos couldn't believe it. An astonished trace of a smile passed across his features as he turned in slow circles, dodging spells, fireballs, and weapons tossed in the air, manipulating every head his mind-reading abilities reached, convincing them they could handle this. Each time he changed the inner workings of another mind, the stronger he felt, the more confidence he grew. They *could* do this. There were so many fighters. And the Defenders weren't the only ones with magical abilities. Many of their warriors had been in battles before, were older and wiser, and had more experience.

So zoned in on his new strategy, Kaos hadn't been paying much attention to the other Defenders and how they were doing with their powers. With them being more united than they ever had before, were the other four feeling just as strong as he currently did? Or were they struggling mentally as he had been not long ago?

The first one he spotted among all the chaos was Rose. She had somehow grown some sort of venomous plant that shot out dangerously fast darts with very pointed tips. These darts flew into a wall of blue fire and disappeared from sight. Rose must have figured out where Yash was hiding—behind his fire.

Pathetic, Kaos thought, shaking his head. Knowing the general location of Yash now, however, he tried his hand at getting a mental signal of him again. With Yash distracted by the poisonous darts, Kaos was finally able to connect to his mind. He knew he had been successful because he could sense the pain Yash felt from Rose's plant. But the pain wore off quickly, much quicker than it would have for a normal person. And once it did, Kaos sensed Yash's mind focusing and sharpening, zeroing in on the fact that he wasn't alone inside his head.

Kaos roared out, more in fury than in pain, as the electric shock jolted through his body once more. He dropped to his knees, furious that Yash had control over him. If he could just keep him distracted by other things while he was trying to get inside his mind, he was sure he could do something that aided in his defeat, whether it be controlling him to cause his own death or anticipating his next moves so that the Defenders could counteract.

Kaos dropped the connection—or maybe Yash forced him out; Kaos wasn't sure which. But the last thing he felt, the last thing he heard inside Yash's head, was the evil entity's sinister laugh. Kaos had barely caught a fleeting glimpse inside Yash's mind before the contact was lost. In that brief moment, he discerned Yash's want for vengeance, for payback. Kaos sensed that Yash was going to do something to make Kaos regret his actions, and that he'd do so by singling out one person in particular, a Defender whom Kaos heard Yash's mind zero in on before Kaos lost contact. An important part of the Defenders. One who was cared about a great deal by all of the other members. Loved by one of them deeply, bonded by blood from another, admired by another, and the last member had been honorably brokenhearted by her. Brokenhearted in a way that didn't make him like her any less, brokenhearted in a way that only made his respect for her grow.

Yash's mind had zeroed in on Amberly.

Kaos looked around for her frantically. The laughter was no longer inside Yash's head; roars across the screams and cries and shouts of the battle rang out through metaphorical stadium speakers, like music to a mosh pit.

The wall of fire that had been there moments ago, Rose's plant shooting poisonous daggers through it, vanished as if it had been sucked right out of the air by someone inhaling a massively deep breath. With the heat gone, it was replaced by a cold feeling. Dread washed over Kaos. But it was different from before, as though he was *forced* to be feeling it, as if Yash was letting him know something terrible was coming.

He saw it in the distance, small at first but steadily, rapidly growing bigger and bigger: a massive ball of blue flame. Not from Trace's sword, not from anyone else's doing except for Yash's.

It was the brilliant blue of the Yarra fire.

"Amberly!" Kaos shouted at the top of his lungs, desperate to find her, to warn her what was about to happen, to protect her from Yash. Once the ball of flames grew to the size of a large boulder, it soared through the vast, neon-lit space as though it had just broken out of powerful restraints holding it back.

"Amberly!"

Why couldn't their powers work on each other at a time like this? How could he make it so that Halo's shield protected Amberly? There wasn't enough time!

"Dad, what are you doing?!" someone's voice shouted through the midst. Everyone had gone mostly to a standstill at the sight of the ball of blue flames, but one person, easily spotted because of how they ran through the stillness, didn't follow suit. Instead, they ran through the crowd, seemingly to the fireball itself. It was Oswald. He was just a villager. He had no particular magic abilities. How did he think he was going to stop this?

"Oswald!" Kaos shouted, wanting to command him to stop, trying to use his mind powers to do so. He had been weakened from the electrocution from Yash and couldn't get a connection to him quickly enough.

"Dad, no!"

Everything happened so fast and so slow all at the same time.

The fireball hurtled toward the direct spot Oswald sprinted to.

When Kaos's eyes reached the trajectory point of both things, he saw their target: Amberly. Oswald had heard Kaos shouting for her, understanding that he knew what was coming. And now he was racing to Amberly's defense.

But there was only one way a plain, powerless human like Oswald could protect her.

"No, wait!" Kaos shouted, reaching out to him. There had to be another way, any other way!

But Kaos couldn't *exactly* command Oswald to stop. He couldn't prevent him from diving in front of Amberly. Doing so would cost Amberly's life, and it was just much too valuable to Kaos for him to risk it.

The fireball struck Oswald with such force that it was akin to swiftly pulling a tablecloth out from underneath a fully set dinner table, and remarkably, none of the glassware or plates atop the table budged. Despite the impact, Oswald remained unmoved as the fireball shot right through him.

And as he was obliterated, the fire of Yarra dimmed, but not entirely. Not in the way Oswald had probably been hoping. The ball of fire exploded through the man and turned into a sort of cloud of flames that enveloped Amberly and then extinguished.

And though Amberly was screaming and writhing around on the ground, and though Oswald's son had dropped to his knees and cried out in a pain that broke Kaos's heart into a million pieces, the battle continued. Yash was not done fighting. He'd never be done fighting. Not until his last dying breath.

More spells soared through the space. Colorful neon lights lit a horrific backdrop. Yash managed to attack many all at once, not even needing to show himself. He could be anything, and he could be nothing. And he could *still* attack.

Kaos wanted nothing more than to just get to Amberly, to just get to that writhing body rolling around on the ground, red neon light glowing underneath her. He started at a terrified sprint, but his path became quickly blocked by two figures who seemingly appeared out of the air.

"Out of the way!" Kaos shouted at them. He barreled into them, trying to shove them aside, but the thin, very tall one of the two had a surprisingly strong grip for somebody so old.

It was Albus. Not *their* Albus, but Albus's best friend. And with him was Gertrude.

"Listen to me!" Albus shouted, his voice grave and serious as he shook Kaos's shoulder. In the blink of an eye, they teleported through the battle arena and were now right next to Amberly's horribly burned body. Suddenly, the other Defenders, Trace, Kire, and Rose, were all there, too. Amberly continued to scream on the ground, begging for somebody to just end it. Kaos was too terrified to even look at her. She was unrecognizable. Burns covered every inch of her body.

Rose sobbed loudly as Albus and Gertrude wrangled them all in. "You need to go and save her right now," Gertrude told them. "You must go!"

"What are you talking about?!" Kire shouted. "How... How are we supposed to leave? How... How can we save her?!"

"Gertrude and I can hold Yash off, but not for long. We are much too old; our magic is too used up to be useful for long. But if you stay here, it'll cost you Amberly's life."

In an attempt to keep his eyes focused on anything other than Amberly, Kaos looked upward, realizing that they were in a sort of bubble in the middle of the battlefield. Weapons and spells and balls of fire and light shot overhead and slammed into an invisible barrier, Halo's shield.

"Oh my God, oh my God, oh my God," Rose sobbed, her shoulders shaking.

"Amberly," Trace whispered, tears streaming down his face too.

"Halo, now!" Albus's voice boomed.

In another blink of an instant, they were off Yash's ship.

23

After Kaos got his bearings, he knew at once where the second Albus had forced them to go. They were in Halo's world. The strange, short, blue bunny figure stood directly by Kaos's side as soon as they touched down on the plush, dark green grass, Amberly arriving in the same state as if she had never even moved, as if Halo's world had just appeared around the spot where she lay dying from her burn wounds.

"Halo!" Kire shouted the second he saw her. "Do something! You have to do something!"

Trace disregarded the bunny man completely and dropped onto his knees next to the love of his life. Amberly's screams were lessening, which Kaos thought should be a good sign but knew it wasn't. She was growing stiller. Her eyes were swelled shut and red, all of her hair burnt clean off. Her skin bubbled and oozed. Her chest rose and fell in quick succession and very faintly.

"I'm afraid I can't do that," Halo said, drooping his head, a carrot dangling out of his mouth. "I'm not a healer. That's not part of my abilities. Albus must have brought you here because he thinks one of *you* can do it."

They all stared around at each other for a moment. Everyone except Amberly.

"We... We can't use our gifts on each other!" Rose cried. "None of us can save her!"

"Amberly, no," Trace said, gripping Amberly's burned hand in his. Tears dripped from his eyes straight onto her chest as he hovered over her in a way that was protective but also desperate.

"Well, he wouldn't have sent you here otherwise..." Halo trailed off, as if thinking. Or maybe he just thought this was hopeless. That there was nothing any of them could do and that Albus had made a mistake.

"I think he knew I would be able to do it."

The voice behind Kaos was soft and masculine and very, very familiar to him.

"A-Albus?" Rose gasped out, choking on her words.

Kaos spun around to see the person he thought he'd never see again. Albus. *Their* Albus.

"How is this even possible?" Kire asked.

"I was about to ask the same thing," Halo replied, giving the old magical being an impressed once over.

"My young friends," Albus said, smiling at all of them fondly as he broke through their circle. "My brave fighters. In a world such as this, so many things are possible."

"Albus," Trace begged, wiping his snotty nose on the back of his hand as he looked up at the old man from down on the ground beside his dying significant other. "Please tell me you can do this. Please tell me you can make her better—I can't lose her, Albus. I just can't!"

Kaos tried to swallow down the lump he felt in his own throat, but it was impossible. His eyes stung. His body trembled. He feared a future that had no Amberly in it, and it was too awful to imagine.

Albus knelt beside Trace, placing an old, wrinkly hand gently on his shoulder. Amberly had grown entirely still. The only sound now was Rose's sobs.

Albus used his other hand to replace the one Trace was using to hold Amberly's, taking it instead in his own. He brought her hand up to his chest and closed his eyes as he pressed her hand against him. Then, even Rose's sobs turned silent.

"We need you, Amberly," Kire whispered. Kaos wiped his eyes, never agreeing with anything Kire had said more in his entire life.

Suddenly, Amberly's body began to glow. A small ember, right in the location of her heart. The tiny fleck, similar to the blue fire that had done this to her, slowly and steadily burned brighter and bigger. Then, in a burst, it spread out across her entire body, mimicking a vein-like pattern as tiny bolts of electricity were being shot through her, visible underneath her burnt flesh. They blazed brilliantly, so bright that Kaos squinted, not wanting to close his eyes for fear of missing what was happening.

After a few seconds, the light faded and disappeared. But what it left in its wake was an entirely different Amberly.

She was healed.

First, even though Albus had let go of her hand and got to his feet, nobody else moved. They all just stared at her.

"Amberly?" Trace asked, his voice soft and hopeful.

Slowly, Amberly's previously burned-off eyelids opened. She cautiously looked around. "What happened?" she asked in a groggy voice, as if she had just woken from a long night of sleep.

"Thank God!" Trace threw his arms around her then, enveloping her in a bear hug, not the slightest bit careful of her possibly weakened state. "I thought I lost you!" He scooped her up in his arms, and even though she looked slightly confused when he kissed her, she kissed him back with passion.

Kaos continued to attempt to keep his eyes dry, but now his tears weren't from sadness; they were from pure elation. He didn't understand how any of this worked and how it was possible, but Amberly was going to live. She had been given another chance, and they couldn't waste it.

Soon enough, everyone's arms were around Amberly, and the Defenders embraced in a large group hug.

"You guys are acting like I just woke from the dead or something," Amberly joked, easing the tension.

"I don't think you realize..." Trace started, but Kaos patted him on the shoulder and shook his head.

"We'll fill her in later."

"Good point."

"Yes, this reunion is quite sweet and all," Albus said to them, causing Amberly's head to snap in his direction.

"Albus? Is that you?" She stood and stepped away from the others, closer to her savior. "Are we all dead?" But then her eyes went to the bunny. "It's you," she said. "So that means—" She looked around herself. "Wait, what are we doing *here*? How are you here, Albus?"

"Oh, just passing the time," he said simply.

"We should probably get back there," Kaos said, clearing his throat. "You guys heard what Albus—the *other* Albus—said. They're not gonna be able to hold off and help in the battle forever. And without them and without us, I'm pretty sure the universe is doomed."

Kire's eyes snapped to Albus. "Can you help us? More than you already have? I know it's asking a lot. But we have to defeat him. We have to win this. We have so many people counting on us. And not just in this realm. In yours, too."

"I am afraid all I can do now is offer my advice."

"Oh boy, here we go," Amberly groaned, talking like Albus had never left. It was oddly comforting to Kaos. Maybe he never really had.

"We'll take anything you can give us," Kire said, shooting his sister a look.

"You're all doing surprisingly well, given the circumstances," Albus said. "However, using your powers the way you are now isn't enough. Kaos, what you're doing with your crown, you all need more of that."

"More of what?" Kire asked. "What was he doing?"

"I was controlling the fighters instead of trying to control Yash," he explained. "I gave them hope and confidence and maybe a bit of fighting knowledge."

"That's really smart," Amberly said, smiling at him. It was so strange to see her acting as though she hadn't nearly just been burned to death, as if seeing her in that horrific state had just been a figment of Kaos's imagination.

"Thanks," Kaos replied.

"Okay then," Rose said, "how can we think more outside the box then?

"The thing about you being a group is that you're supposed to stick together," Albus replied. "Combine your powers. You may not be able to use them on each other, but you can use them together."

"I... I think we can do that," Kaos replied. Already, he had an idea forming in his head of how they could unite their strengths.

"I knew you would," Albus said. "It seems that you, Kaos, my friend, have found your way out of the darkness."

"I... I have," Kaos replied. "And I'm never going back to that place again."

Albus's eyes peered into his as if he was trying to read his mind. Kaos had no doubt that the old man could.

Thank you, he silently told him. *Thank you for saving her.*

24

On top of the hill inside the mind and world of Halo, Albus turned away from the Defenders and gazed upon an expansive meadow disappearing into the setting sun. He sighed heavily.

Rose was the first to follow him. "What is it?" she asked him.

"How much time do we have before the other Albus and Gertrude are no longer able to continue fighting for us?" Kire asked, trailing behind his girlfriend, both of them walking timidly up behind Albus as if they were worried about disturbing him too deeply as he stood there in his own thoughts. Something troubled Albus. Kaos could see it from where he stood next to his two best friends. He glanced at them, watching the loving way Trace and Amberly looked at each other despite everything going on outside of this world. It was easy to forget about all the other horrors in a place like this. It was so peaceful, so free, so dreamlike. Just like Trace thought he could spend the rest of his life inside the Albus realm, living as a knight in a fancy homestead with a pretty fairy by his side, Kaos thought he could just as easily stay here forever. It would be simple, effortless. The rest of his life would be a breeze.

"I'm afraid I have something I must show you," Albus said,

seeming to ignore Kire and Rose as he continued to gaze out into the distance. Kaos was almost unsure if he was even talking to them or if he was addressing somebody from beyond. He didn't know how any of this stuff worked. He wondered if Albus himself even knew.

"What is it?" Kaos asked, still hanging back. There was something about Albus's presence that still intimidated him, that caused him to want to keep his distance. Even though the man seemed like a fun-loving, easy-going, carefree kind of guy, the fact that he could act this way but still be so powerful, that he still had the power to destroy something in seconds, made Kaos slightly uneasy. And maybe he was still slightly resentful of some of the things Albus had pointed out about him in the past. Were those things he had said true? Yes. Did that mean Kaos appreciated hearing them? Not entirely.

"I think it might be best if you just watch this first," Albus explained. He waved his hand in an arcing motion through the air, and through his magic, a sort of screen appeared, floating there like they were at a movie theater, waiting for the viewing to start.

"Whoa," Halo called. "You're gonna have to teach me how to do that."

Albus didn't reply to him. Apparently, this was not the time for jokes. Why Halo wasn't understanding that was a mystery to Kaos.

Just as Albus had been able to project himself to appear in front of the Defenders when he had been alive, back in his Albus realm when they were in their own realm, it appeared as though Albus could also project their realm to them no matter where they were. He had told them some engineer crafted something fancy to enable him to do so. Evidently, now that he was dead, he could do whatever he wanted. No engineer required.

Their world came into view. Kaos could recognize the streets of Montgomery, even when they were in their current state, which wasn't good. As though a drone was slowly floating through the clouds, giving a bird's-eye view of their town, Kaos's mouth dropped open as he stared at the destruction. Fires everywhere. Cars totaled. Buildings in ruins. Parts of the earth looked as though they had been split open all the way to its core.

"No," Rose breathed.

"Holy—" Amberly said, cutting herself off.

"You see, what you don't realize is that while you are on Yash's ship, fighting this battle, there is still destruction happening in your realm outside of the sinkhole." Albus finally turned to look at all of them, each one in turn, his eyes dark and serious. Were they always so dark? Hadn't they been completely white when he was alive? His beard and hair had been a bit more disheveled when he was alive, too. Here in this world, everything was neatly kept. His curly hair, which resembled a French wig, was neatly in place. He wore a gown of the deepest cobalt blue. He looked something like a god to Kaos.

"I don't get it," Trace barked, balling his fists at his side as he watched the projection. "How can he do so much damage in so many different places all at the same time? I thought we were holding him off from all of that."

"I know you did; that is why I wanted to show you this. And I'm afraid it is only about to get worse."

"How?" Amberly asked.

The projection changed. It zoomed out even further as if the drone had flown out of the atmosphere, the entire Earth visible from space. But then, it zoomed back in, only this time, to a completely different continent. To a country in Europe. It zoomed in more and more as if they were on Google Maps, with a live feed. It stopped zooming when it reached the boundaries of a city, and then it slowly hovered through the sky, showcasing the streets like it had done in Montgomery.

And it was all the same here. In this random town in Europe, buildings had been obliterated. Little fires dotted the map and filled the air with smoke. Kaos could hear screams this time, too.

Panicked people running through the streets. People shouting about the end of the world.

"It's spreading," Kire said matter-of-factly, as if more to himself than anyone else. As if he hadn't even realized he was speaking out loud.

"It's not the only thing that's spreading," Albus agreed. It zoomed out once more. But Kaos didn't know if he could handle seeing another decimated village or town. How many places across Earth looked like that? A fourth of them? Half of them? Nearly *all* of them? He shuddered.

When it zoomed in again, a massive wall of blue hurtled toward a busy skyscraper-filled city, like a tsunami about to slam down on everything. Only, this wasn't a tsunami.

It was a massive wall of blue fire.

"The fire of Yarra!" Kaos shouted. "It's going to wipe out that whole city!"

"It can, and it will, and it'll happen soon. It's exactly what Yash wants. And he wants you to remain unaware that he can still do all of this while you're on his ship, trying to end him. He doesn't know that I'm showing you this now. He won't know when you return."

"So... we have to go back then," Amberly said, standing up straight and rolling her shoulders back. "We have to go back right now and stop him!"

"Are you sure?" Trace asked her, giving her a pointed look. "Are you sure you're ready?"

"What are you talking about? I feel stronger than I ever have. When we're united like this, we're unstoppable. I know we can stop him. I know we can fix this. We can make everything right."

"We stick together this time then," Kire said. Everyone stared at Kaos. Even Halo and Albus, as though they were curious about what he had to say about it. The leader of the Defenders, about to give his instructions. Possibly for the last time.

He nodded sternly. "Agreed. We stick together, and we use our abilities together. We fight, and we fight, and we stop at nothing."

"Until the very end," Amberly said. They all repeated after her.

"Until the very end."

"You feel that?" Albus said, stepping back to them, the projection disappearing out of the sky. They all stared at him. "You feel it spreading through your bodies, out through the tips of your fingers and toes?"

Kaos could feel it. The same feeling he had before. That buzzing sensation.

"I think I do," Trace replied.

"Same," Rose agreed. Kire and Amberly nodded.

"You are finally united," Albus informed them. "You five are finally whole."

"All right, Halo," Kire said, looking over at the bunny. "We're ready."

"Wait!" Rose called. They turned to her to see her looking at Albus. "Will we be able to see you again after all of this? If we survive? Can we come back in here whenever we need to meet with you?"

"It would be nice if that were possible," Albus told her. "Like I said, anything can happen here. But if Yash is defeated, then there is no need for Defenders, for there will be peace. And with that peace, you will no longer need your abilities."

"What?" Kaos gasped incredulously.

"You'll do great," Albus reassured them. Then he nodded at Halo.

"Hang on a second!" Kaos called, but it was too late.

They were back on the battlefield. The second they reappeared and Kaos's eyes found the other Albus and Gertrude, the two disappeared as if they had done a flip-flop. As if Halo had pulled them inside the same way the Defenders had been pulled in. Albus and Gertrude had done all they could, and now it was the Defenders' turn to fight Yash, to end this once and for all.

"Halo's still got a shield on us," Kire said to the others. "Kaos, what do we do?"

"Rose," Kaos said, clapping his hands together. "Do you think you could manipulate some plants to turn them into animals? Ones that you can control?"

"I've never tried it before, but maybe."

He nodded. Then he turned his head to Trace. "Trace, can you set the whole thing on fire, creating an untouchable beast?"

Trace nodded, his eyes sparkling with excitement. "Definitely."

"Let's try that first. Kire, focus on defending our troops. Can you direct Halo's shield out to whoever you see needing it?"

"I'm on it."

"Amberly, use your telekinesis to keep things out of everyone's way!"

She nodded, looking focused and sharp. Albus had healed her completely—and then some, it seemed.

"I'll keep helping the other fighters be better," Kaos said. "Now go!"

They all did as they were told, the group breaking away and the shield dissipating, immersing them back in the center of it all. Shouts and cries continued. Blood was spilled. Lives were ended. And yet, the Defenders kept fighting. Kaos's idea worked—Rose used a bunch of plants she produced out of the air to entangle into a grizzly bear, one that was on fire and fighting against the blue flames of Yarra as it growled and swung its mighty claws. It worked well at first, the troops getting a moment of reprieve as Yash had to focus more attention on attacking the flaming grizzly bear. But with each passing moment, the blue flames of Yarra grew bigger, taking up more space, making Kaos's skin feel as though he had jumped into a Jacuzzi. He was hot, but not in a way that was at all relaxing.

The blue fire overtook the Defenders' flaming bear, swallowing it up and ruining the plan.

"It's okay!" Kaos called to the others. They remained in each other's vicinity so that they could continue to get direction from their leader. "Amberly, whatever you can find, send it hurtling in

Yash's direction, somewhere behind Yarra. He hides behind it! And Trace, light her projectiles on fire!"

They nodded to show they understood and acted quickly. Amberly sent one object flying through the blackness after another with great speed, almost to the point where Trace had trouble keeping up with lighting them on fire as they hurled over the blue flames and disappeared behind them. Kaos didn't attempt another read on Yash's mind to see if he had been hit because he couldn't lose his focus. He wanted to keep helping his troops and guiding his teammates.

He watched with relief as the blue fire slightly diminished. It had to be a sign that the projectiles were weakening Yash. Kaos looked into the blackness beyond them with hope.

But the hope disappeared just as swiftly as the flaming fireballs suddenly soared back in their direction, as if they were boomerangs.

"Kire!" Kaos yelled. He didn't need to say anything else before Kire shot Halo open in the direction where the flaming objects soared toward everyone, and as though the shield could multiply into fifty smaller ones, they acted as umbrellas, and the fireballs bounced right off them, falling into the once again powerful blue flames and disappearing.

Crap.

The sounds of battle were growing quieter around them. People were weakening. Their numbers were dwindling. The loss of Oswald, their troop's leader, and his heartbroken, terrified son left behind, had broken their spirits. Had lessened their confidence. He could feel it inside their minds as he tried to control them to keep pushing onward. Even though the Defenders felt strong, their fighters did not. Their fighters were tired.

"There's gotta be something else we can do!" Kaos shouted to himself. Something that combined *all* of their abilities!

He jumped and turned to the others when he had his eureka moment.

Things were about to get serious.

"Okay!" Kaos shouted as Halo deflected something centimeters away from hitting him square in the chest. He took a moment to regroup and catch his breath. "Okay," he tried again, dusting himself off. "This is going to take all of us, and I have no idea if it'll work. But we've got to try!"

"Hurry up and tell us what to do!" Amberly shouted.

"Trace, I need you to throw out a fireball. Amberly, I need you to catch it telekinetically and keep it steady. Rose, I need you to give it everything you have and create the biggest monster you can think of. Something huge. Got it? It needs to envelop the fireball without extinguishing it, okay?!"

Rose nodded. "I can do it."

"I know you can."

They jumped into action. Using his sword, Trace shot a fireball of his own into the sky. Amberly caught it telepathically, and it hovered like a miniature sun. Vines and branches, larger than anything Kaos had ever seen Rose make, circled the fireball, keeping it glowing bright as it morphed into something better than Kaos could've imagined—a life-size freaking dragon.

It was magnificent.

"Can you control this thing?!" Kaos asked Rose. He noticed the blood trickling down her nose as she used everything she could. But she didn't look to be in any pain. She didn't look to be weakening. She hardly even seemed to notice the blood.

"I've got it!"

"Great!" Kaos called. "Now, make something that'll help me climb on top of it!"

"Are you crazy?!" Amberly shouted to him.

Kaos ignored her. "Rose, come on! Our troop is weakening! We have to hurry!"

She nodded, and a particularly thick vine snaked through the atmosphere, picking up Kaos as though he were as light as a feather and dropping him onto the back of the fire-breathing dragon plant. It was easy for him to keep his grip on the thing, for he had many branches and vines to choose from. His feet sunk into soft greenery as though he were strapping in to ride a stationary bike at the gym. He was secure, and he was ready to fight.

"Kire!" Rose called, her voice slightly strained now. "Make sure Halo protects both of them!"

Kaos was sure she was referring to him and the dragon.

Rose guided the beast toward the blue flames. The dragon was so large that it towered even over that. And up high where he sat, Kaos could see Yash. Finally, a single entity. A single being. His thin, tall body, his slit for eyes. The glowing red inside of them. His thin, practically invisible eyebrows narrowed in concentration and confusion at what he was seeing peeking up over his precious blue fire.

This was it. This was their chance. Outside of this, an entire city full of millions of people was about to be engulfed by Yarra—if it hadn't already started to engulf it. There were no other options. There was no more time. It had run out, and this was all they had left.

It was time to end this.

"Rose!" Kaos shouted above the roar of the dragon. "Trace! Fire! Now!"

A stream of flames flew through the air from the tip of Trace's blade and into the fireball that acted as the core of the dragon, right into its stomach, like a spider's web being threaded. The stream of flames remained steady, which was something Kaos had never seen Trace's sword do before. Trace's fire was feeding the dragon, keeping the ball alive as the beast started to deeply inhale.

"You'll never stop me. You can't save this world!" Yash's voice boomed. "You cannot stop the most powerful being in existence! Yarra's fire will not be extinguished!"

"I don't know about you, sir," Kaos shouted at him sarcastically over the blue flame as the dragon continued a long, slow, massive inhale. "But it sounds to me like you're trying to convince yourself more than you're trying to convince us."

There was a moment of suspension when the dragon's inhale ceased. A moment of stillness. A moment where even Yash couldn't come up with a response. Then, as the dragon roared louder than anything Yash could shout with his booming voice, the most powerful, brilliant red blast of fire shot out of the dragon's mouth and fought against the blue flames of Yarra. The red fire made the blue flames look like the small, weak, teardrop-shaped flames at the end of candle wicks. In comparison to the crimson-red fire that shot out of the dragon's mouth in a cloud almost as big as the dragon itself, the fire of Yarra was nothing. And nothing that fire became as the Defenders' fire swallowed it hole.

With Yarra extinguished, the dragon's flame's shape changed. It morphed, encircling the great and powerful Yash, creating a cube. It took Kaos a second to realize it, but it was locking him inside of a fiery cage.

"No!" boomed a furious voice. Yash was trapped. And as distracted as he was trying to figure out a way to fix this, Kaos had an easy way back in his mind. Yash was so desperate—Kaos could see it so clearly. So desperate that he hardly even acknowledged Kaos was there inside his mind at all. He didn't do anything to stop him. He was too busy trying to think of a way to escape. But the fire the Defenders had created—Yash referred to it as something strange as Kaos read his thoughts—Ignis Vortis—it was his weakness. It was something only a united group of Defenders could create. Kaos learned Yash had worked so hard to keep the teens from morphing into one united force. How had this happened to him?

Maybe if you had a heart of your own, you'd understand better how to prevent love from forming, Kaos thought into Yash's mind. This angered Yash, causing him to become more attuned to Kaos's presence.

And just like that, the electric shock shot back through Kaos's body.

He shouted out in pain and gripped the dragon for dear life. In his desperation, Yash changed his target. *Screw the Ignis Vortis's cage,* Yash thought. He just wanted to get this little twerp out of his head.

The pain was unlike anything Kaos had ever felt. His head screamed. His limbs were on fire.

"Hang on!"

Somehow, a voice broke through his agony. It was Trace's.

"Just hang in there!" Trace yelled up to his friend.

"You got this, Kaos! Don't give up!" Rose's voice called next. She sounded strong despite the toll controlling this magnificent beast must've been taking on her. If *she* could be so strong, surely Kaos could be, too, right?

"Lead us out of this mess!" Amberly shouted next.

Kaos kept screaming through the pain, his eyes squeezed shut, his grip so tight on the vines that they cut into his skin. It felt like a nice massage compared to the pain of the rest of his body.

"Halo can only make a physical shield!" Kire explained. "You've got to fight this on your own, Kaos!"

Among all of it, Kaos could hear Yash laughing again, in that sinister way that made it seem as though *he* had the upper hand. As though he had everything under control, Kaos was going to be dead in an instant, and Yarra would be back in full force in no time.

Through the pain, Kaos started experiencing memories. Ones of himself chasing Kire through the woods with Trace and Amberly back when they were enemies. Ones from when he realized he thought of Amberly as more than just a friend. Ones from when he ruined his friendship with Trace and thought it was over for good. To when they killed Jago and Heno, and when they killed Rezin.

Yash was taking over Kaos's mind. Pushing back. Kaos's mouth opened, but not of his own doing. Yash was somehow controlling him. *Making* him speak.

"I—" he choked out, trying so hard to fight against it but unable to stop himself. "I caused Rezin's death!"

Stop! he thought loudly in his head. But of course, Yash wasn't going to listen to him. "It's my fault! I let Rezin in! I let him see! I wanted him to see our plans!"

No, that's not true! I did everything I could to prevent it!

Kaos waited for what came next. For his friends to turn on him. For them to change their minds and start cheering on Yash to end Kaos's life instead.

But it didn't happen.

"We don't care about that!" Amberly shouted.

"Any of it!" Rose added.

"Don't let him do this to you!" Trace called. "You're the strongest dude I know! And that's saying a lot, coming from me!"

They... They weren't mad at him? They didn't feel betrayed? They didn't long for their revenge?

"We're united!" Kire called. "We're stronger *together*! Remember that, Kaos! Get him out! End this! You have to do it!"

Kaos shouted as he used every ounce of strength he had to push against Yash inside of his mind. To shove him out. Everything hurt. Everything screamed at him to stop trying. But he kept going anyway. When he got back inside of Yash's head, he could hear his thoughts again. *How is this happening?!* Yash thought angrily. *Why don't they demand revenge?! Why can't I break them?!*

We're stronger together.

Even though it felt like Kaos's head was going to split right open as pain exploded inside every limb of his body, he pushed harder than ever, completely blacking out and losing control of everything around him. All that mattered was Yash. Thinking with all he could, as loudly as he could, he bellowed the command inside of Yash's mind.

It's the end for you, Yash, he thought to himself after.

"No!"

Kaos couldn't tell if the scream was in his head or out loud. Yash tried to fight back, but lifted up by his friends, who were his family, Kaos was stronger than ever. As much as Yash tried to fight against Kaos's powerful mind control, his arms extended outward. They reached for the flaming bars of the cage.

Do it, Kaos pushed, feeling as though he was now outside of himself, watching the scene from the same drone-like object that had shown them all the projections inside of Halo's world.

With the final scream, Yash's fingers forcefully curled around the prison bars created by *Ignis Vortis,* and in seconds, Yash's entire body was ablaze.

And as he turned to ash, everything inside Kaos's mind finally grew silent.

25

W hen Kaos opened his eyes again, he was no longer riding a red fire-breathing dragon made from plants. He was on the ground, a puddle of neon blue surrounding his body. The dragon was nowhere in sight, likely since they no longer had any use for it. Looking around, Kaos noticed they were still on Yash's ship of darkness, in between realms, even though Yash no longer existed. All of those near him refused to move a single muscle; hardly anyone even blinked. It was as though no one could really believe it. As though they all had the same question. Was Yash really gone?

The only thing that made Kaos also question it was the fact that they were still here. How could Yash's ship exist if there was no great, evil entity to control it?

When the Defenders reached Kaos's side, they helped him to his feet. None of them seemed to know what to do next. Kaos cleared his throat, glad the pain he had felt moments ago had subsided and morphed into a dull ache. His body was sore and tired, but he was okay. And Yash was dead.

"What..." Trace began, looking stunned at the fact that it was over. "What happens now?"

Before Kaos could open his mouth to say that he didn't have the slightest clue, the black nothingness above them opened up, and a rainstorm showered down one magical beast after another. Werewolves. Witches. Banshees. Trolls. Giants. They slammed to the ground in a swirl of neon, landing all in the same position, on one knee with their heads bent low.

Everyone gasped and watched as more and more appeared, one after the other, all landing in the same formation. Kaos scanned his surroundings, quickly realizing that they were all facing the same direction. They were all facing him.

"What is this?" Kaos asked of their submissive state. "What's going on right now?"

"Dude," said Trace, slapping a hand onto Kaos's back. "I think these are Yash's minions. And I think... I think they're sort of your minions now."

"What?" Kaos couldn't comprehend it; it couldn't be possible. And yet, hundreds of magical creatures bowed before him. Not angrily, but with expressions of acceptance. Acceptance of what? Of him as their leader? Was this really happening?

"You look confused," a deep voice said from behind. Kaos and the others turned to find Albus had returned, without Gertrude this time, and with a bruised body and a cane to help him walk toward them.

"Albus," Kaos said, "are you all right?"

"Is Kaos Miles really going to be such a caring leader?" Albus asked with a glimmer of mischief in his eyes.

"Leader?" Kaos asked. "You're not serious."

"I am," Albus replied. "You defeated Yash after centuries of his evil rule."

"But it... it wasn't just me. It was all of us. I don't understand. And what about the world outside of here? How bad is it?"

"There will be quite a bit of work to do to clean up and repair your realm. But hope is not lost."

"I... I still don't understand."

"Everyone gave you aid in the fight against Yash, yes," Albus explained, "but in the end, there was only one person who truly put a stop to Yash once and for all. And my dear boy, that is you."

"So, you're saying..." Kaos was in complete disbelief. "All of these... All of them... I am in charge of?"

"That would be correct."

"But I... I'm just a kid."

"A kid who has done what no one else could, despite many attempts. Stop fighting it, will you? I'm terribly tired. All I want is a nice cup of tea and a comfortable bed for the night. You've come a long way from the boy you used to be. Before me now stands a strong man, one ready to do right by the world. Right by those he cares about. You will do great things, Kaos."

"Hang on." He ran a hand through his heavily disheveled hair. "But didn't any of you hear what I said earlier? I didn't even want to say it, but... But Yash made me. I—I am the reason Rezin died. I am the reason we had to have this battle in the first place. All those lives that were lost during this... it's my fault. H-how can I be appointed some promising leader after what I've done?"

"We heard you," Amberly acknowledged. Kaos thought she should be staring at him with fiery hate in her eyes. Instead, they were soft, kind, and forgiving. "But how could you have possibly known when you tried to get into Rezin's head that he would be able to retaliate and get into yours? None of us could have seen it coming."

"Well, none of us except for maybe Halo," Kire called. With Rose's arm hugged around his waist, he held Halo open, giving it a disapproving stare and head shake.

"I.... I don't know what to say," Kaos breathed.

Rose piped up next. "Despite being a little bit rough around the edges, you turned out to be a really good leader, Kaos. We would have never gotten where we are without you."

Kaos smiled at her, his eyes flitting to Kire.

"What?" Kire asked, looking around at the others. "Oh, is it my turn to say something encouraging to him?"

Rose nudged him.

"Kidding," he said before fixing his gaze back on Kaos. "I agree with Rose. I would have never lasted as the leader. I would never be able to think of some of the things you thought of that helped us save an entire universe. That's...pretty incredible if you ask me."

"Thanks, Kire."

Kaos turned to his "minions." But he didn't like the term. It made them sound too evil. Kaos didn't want that for them. He didn't want to use his newfound power for darkness.

"Uh, you can all stop bowing now?" he called to the magical beasts. "Can one of you—here, how about you?" He pointed to a troll nearest him. The giant creature bore a fierce expression and had bulging muscles. "Can you tell me where exactly you all just came from? Why were none of you here when we were all fighting your previous leader?"

The troll cleared his throat, but he was so massive it sounded like rolling thunder. "My lord," he addressed Kaos.

Lord? How is this real?

The troll, with dark green skin covered in unsightly red boils, continued. "We simply existed when and if Yash wanted us to. Then and only then. Otherwise, we were here, but not in a way that could be seen, heard, or felt. He didn't want to call upon us in the battle against his biggest adversaries. He wanted to do it alone. A bit proud, that thing was."

The teens smirked around at each other. Yash had greatly underestimated them. And thank God he had.

"I see." Kaos stood as tall as possible, wanting to appear mature and respectable in front of everyone. He was a leader now. He supposed he needed to act like it. "So, then, if I don't want you to remain here in this... this place, then where exactly am I supposed to bring you all? You don't exactly fit in in my world."

"If they don't intend to cause us any further harm," Albus

responded, "if you have every intention of being a fair and just leader of these creatures, my realm would be a welcome place for them. I have the perfect plot of land in mind for where we can begin construction of your great kingdom."

"An entire kingdom?" Trace whispered, his eyes bugging out of his head. "Dude—that's sick!"

"But I don't want to live in your realm," Kaos said automatically. Thinking it felt a bit harsh, he afterward added, "No offense."

Albus sighed. "You know how time works between the realms, do you not?"

The five teenagers stared around at each other. Simultaneously, they all responded, "No," and then burst into a small fit of laughter.

Albus's eyes went upward toward the abyss where a sky or roof should be. "What I am trying to say is that it's quite possible for you to do both, my child. Or should I say, my lord."

"No, definitely don't say that," Kaos replied, shaking his head repeatedly.

"In any case, I think this has been quite enough for now. Don't you all agree? We're all tired. We have... fallen heroes waiting to be returned to their families. As time goes on, Kaos, you'll understand and accept your new role on a much deeper level. For now, I beg of you five to go home and be the teenagers you were always supposed to be before you stumbled upon those gifts. Say farewell to them, for you will not be needing them any longer."

After Albus's last word, the gifts of the Defenders all started to glow. Amberly's magnificent gauntlet. Rose's powerful pendant. Trace's flaming sword. The crown on Kaos's head. And Halo.

The brightness of their gifts grew more and more blinding until they were one ball of gleaming white light.

Then, they were gone.

"I...I didn't even get to say goodbye," Kire said in a low, gloomy voice.

"The gifts have served their purpose," Albus assured him. "Now, get back to Earth. I'll lead these creatures to their new home and work on the repair of your realm. Come back to the Albus realm when you're ready, Kaos. We'll be there awaiting your direction and guidance."

Kaos looked at his friends.

"I was hoping there'd be reasons for us to have to keep paying visits to the Albus realm," Amberly said, shooting him a wry smile.

"With Yash out of the way, I can finally spend some free time getting a closer look at all the weird plants there!" Rose cried gleefully, beaming at him before adding, "And assisting *you,* of course, *my lord.*"

"You're gonna need an adviser!" Kire called to Kaos, looking truly happy for him that Kaos had been handed this opportunity.

Their gifts were what connected them before. Their gifts were their only common ground. But even without them, Kaos couldn't imagine any single one of them not forever being a part of his life.

It seemed they felt the same.

"And we'll all be right there with you," Trace added, giving his best friend an encouraging smile as the others nodded along. "Every step of the way."

AUTHOR'S NOTE

Dear Beloved Reader,

Thank you so much for joining me in this epic conclusion with The Unlikely Defenders from Kaos's point of view in The Untimely Champions.

I truly hope that you enjoyed it! If you did, I would be so grateful if you would consider leaving a review. Reviews help other readers find my work, so a review is very valuable to me.

I really hope you enjoyed this series as much as I enjoyed sharing it with you. Also, feel free to check out my other books and series!

https://swiy.co/UnlikelyDefenders

Visit my website at LilySkyy.com and interact with me on social media. Did you know that you could support me directly by purchasing books directly from my website instead of a third-party store? There's also awesome merch available for each of my series. Also, make sure to sign up for my mailing list to be the first to know about new releases and special happenings such as previews and give-a-ways!

I love getting feedback from my readers, and if you'd like to stay in touch (or discuss my books), join me over at the Lily Skyy Readers' Group. I'd also love to connect with you on Instagram, TikTok, and Twitter! Feel free to reach out to me directly via email at social@lilyskyy.com.

Again, I thank you for reading, and I can't wait to join you on the next adventure!

With heartfelt sincerity,

Lily Skyy